WELCOME [illegible]RADISE

B CROWHURST

ISBN: 9798542305905
Cover design by Design Bunnies

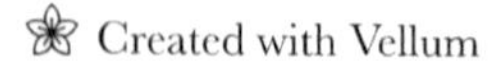

I would like to dedicate this book to my Nan who sadly passed away while I was writing this book. I like to think a little of her tenacity and vibrant spirit worked its way onto these pages.

Alex

My name is Alex Andrews and I own The Paradise Hotel, one of the most luxurious hotels in all of Spain. How I came to be so fortunate is a story for another day, but needless to say I am one lucky son-of-a-bitch.

You'd be surprised what goes on within these walls and there's not much that escapes my attention. I make it my business to know.

Do you know what I see here more than anything else? Love. Not necessarily the seedy type of love you probably associate with hotels where strangers go at it like rabbits, in a room they booked just for the night. (Although I can't deny that happens here as well.) But all kinds of love. The love between families, friends and lovers. Birth, marriage, death, and everything in between.

You want to see love in its many forms? Work in the hospitality business long enough and you'll see it all. These particular tales of love all took place during one eventful month that I hold personally dear to my own heart.

Welcome to Paradise…

Claire

OCEAN'S APART

ARRIVING AT THE PARADISE HOTEL, I can see now the photos in the brochure don't do it justice. This place is breathtakingly beautiful. The hotel entrance looks out straight onto the golden beach with sand and waves for as far as the eye can see in both directions.

Maybe Tony actually got something right for a change. My husband of eight years suggested we book this trip away to Spain in a last ditch attempt to save our failing marriage. *Where is he anyway?* I turn back to the taxi that just dropped us off to see what's taking so long with the bags. *Typical.* He's not even got them out of the boot yet; he's on the phone again.

I huff and stomp over to the taxi, retrieving the bags myself and apologising in what little Spanish I know to the taxi driver. He just smiles politely, he's in no hurry as the meter is still running.

Tony ends his call and hurries over to take the heaviest suitcase. One look at my face tells him I'm less than impressed that this is how the holiday has started.

"Sorry darling, it was urgent work stuff. I had to take it."

I roll my eyes. "Don't you always," I snap back sarcastically.

I pick up the smaller bags and march purposefully off in the direction of the foyer.

An hour later and we have finished checking in and unpacking our things. We've barely said two words to each other since we arrived. It seems to be the way things are now. We go through our days barely tolerating each other and only communicating when we absolutely have to. It's not that either of us wants it this way, but neither of us knows how to fix it.

I pour myself a glass of wine from the mini bar and take a seat on the balcony. I can't decide what's more spectacular, the view or the hotel itself. Our room is made up of luxurious fabrics and clean, white lines. Nothing like our cluttered house back home. We both live such busy lives that the house, and each other, get neglected.

"Claire, do you want to come down and explore the resort with me?" Tony's voice interrupts my train of thought.

"No thanks, I'm pretty tired. I think I'll just chill here for a bit."

I see his shoulders visibly drop in disappointment. *I don't know why I constantly push him away like this.* It's almost become a habit.

"Ok, well I'll see you later for dinner then." He gives me a weak smile before leaving.

What the hell is wrong with me? It's like I'm hell bent on sabotaging our marriage, and I don't even really know why.

I take a large sip from my wine glass and close my eyes. The warm breeze blows wisps of hair round my face, and the heat from the setting sun soaks into my cheeks. It's nice to be able to relax. I don't really do it much. My high-pressure job at the law firm takes up most of my time and energy. There's not a lot of room for anything else, including Tony. *Maybe that's where we've gone wrong?* He's just as much to blame as I am, though. He eats, sleeps, and breathes his job at the bank, too.

Looking down at the beach below, I can see couples and families all enjoying themselves and each other's company. *And yet here we both are, in paradise, still separate and still miserable. Time to take action,* I tell myself assertively.

I drain the remainder of my wine and make my way downstairs to find Tony and take him up on his offer of exploring the resort together. One of us needs to take the first step to building bridges, and I was too stubborn and pig-headed to realise he already had.

This place is huge, I don't really know where to look for him. I noticed on my way out of the room that he, surprisingly, left his mobile on the side, so I can't even call him to see where he is. I decide to start with the beach, he's pretty outdoorsy when he gets the chance, so maybe that's where he's gone.

With my sandals in one hand, I stroll barefoot along the sand, absorbing the idyllic surroundings and atmosphere. There's a young couple chasing each other along the beach. They can't be much older than seventeen at the most. Smiling and laughing, they fall tangled up in the sand together. *I remember those days. What happened to them?*

I walk a fair distance along the beach, but there's no sign of Tony, so I head back inside to try the restaurant and bar. The longer I've spent walking alone with my thoughts, the more I've convinced myself that we do have something worth saving. We loved each other once, we just have to remember why.

The bar is an impressive marble strip that wraps around the edge of the restaurant, separating it from the tropical pool area. Everything here has been flawlessly designed to exude luxury. Tony and I may both be married to our jobs rather than each other, but it does allow us to afford places like this.

I recognise Tony's laugh before I spot him. All the warm and fuzzy feelings that had started to creep back in towards him are instantly snuffed out like a candle flame when I see him. He's sat at the bar with some floozy wrapped around his shoulders. They're both laughing at something she just said. *To be honest, I haven't seen him look that happy in years.* The thought only makes my blood boil even more. The woman is wearing a tight red dress that fits like a glove over her tanned curves and her long blonde hair cascades down her back in golden waves. I try to think back to the last time I wore full make-up and did my hair, or a dress for something other than work and I can't. *Shit, how did we fall this far?*

The truth is I'm hurt and I'm mad. So, so mad. I'm just not sure who I'm mad at. I stand watching them for a minute as they laugh and joke and she paws at my husband's arm. I think she's touched him more in the last five minutes than I have in the last five months. Standing there like an idiot, I'm contemplating which way to handle the situation. The way I see it, I have two choices. I either go storming over there like a mad woman and confront them both, causing an embarrassing scene for everyone, or I walk away and speak to him later. Option one is less than ideal, but option two will leave me wondering for the rest of the evening whether or not my husband found something with this woman that he no longer finds in me.

Before I make the decision, it's taken out of my hands. Tony looks up and sees me from across the bar. He instantly stops laughing and puts some distance between himself and the woman. I just stare at him, and he just stares at me. There is so much we both need to say to one another, but we never allow ourselves to indulge in the emotion of it all. Silent, angry tears start to roll down my cheeks. I never cry. I haven't cried since we were told we couldn't have kids two years ago.

Fight or flight kicks in and for the first time in a long time I fly. Not wanting anyone to see me cry, least of all Tony, I turn and flee back to our room. I run along the corridors, narrowly avoiding unsuspecting guests, and jump in the elevator. By the time I reach the fourth floor and swipe the key card, my cheeks are streaked with rivers of tears.

I know I'm majorly overreacting. *He was just talking to her.* It's not like I found them in bed together. But somehow, this feels even worse. It's almost as if the simple act of finding joy in the company of others when he finds so little in mine is the most hurtful betrayal of all. *You only have yourself to blame for this.* How long did I really think I could keep pushing him away for before he actually left?

No sooner do I reach the other side of the room when I hear the door open behind me. Tony comes storming in with his hands up in front of him defensively.

"Claire, listen. It wasn't how it looked."

"Oh really? So, it didn't look like you were having fun with that woman and enjoying her falling all over you?" I attempt to wipe some of the ruined make-up from my face with a tissue.

"At least she noticed me," he mumbles under his breath.

"What did you say?"

"You heard me. You don't even see me half the time, Claire! And when you do, you look at me like something you just stepped in!"

Tony very rarely raises his voice, so when he does, I know I've really pushed a button. I recoil from his words. *Am I really that bad?*

"How would you know how I look at you? You're always working!" I don't know why I'm throwing back such pathetic defenses; I know deep down that he's right.

Tony huffs in exasperation and rakes his fingers through his hair.

"Yes, do you know what? You're absolutely right. I *was* enjoying talking to Michelle downstairs. For the first time in a really long time, someone actually noticed me and enjoyed my company. It was fun, Claire, remember that?" He grabs a scotch from the mini-bar and pours it over some ice.

"Would you have slept with her if I hadn't come down and interrupted your 'fun?'" I sarcastically use air quotes to accentuate my ridiculous point.

"You can't seriously be asking me that?"

I fold my arms indignantly across my chest, waiting for an answer. *God, you're so pathetic, Claire. Give the guy a damn break.*

"No Claire, of course I wouldn't have slept with her! My marriage vows mean something to me. Why do you think I'm still here?!" he shouts before knocking back the glass of scotch in one gulp.

"I don't know. Why *are* you still here?" His face softens, and he looks more sad than angry.

He's silent for a minute, as if deciding on the best response to my question. "Because we loved each other once. We were happy. Call me crazy, but I like to think we could be again. I think I'll go for a swim and give you some space to think about what it is you want," he says, deflated.

Tony grabs his sunglasses and leaves me all alone in our room. *Nice one, Claire. You royally fucked that up.*

I decide to change into my lounge shorts and vest top and crawl into bed. I seem to have lost my appetite anyway and maybe Tony's right. Time to think might be exactly what I need.

Olivia

INFERNO

"GUESS WHO?" I whisper close to his ear as I clamp my hands over his eyes and nibble on his earlobe. Diego smiles sexily and turns towards me in my arms.

I met Diego five days ago at the hotel spa when he gave me the massage of my life. I came to Spain on a girl's holiday with my three friends but after meeting Diego last week, we've spent almost every available minute together, much to my friends' annoyance.

The girls had booked me in for a back massage as a birthday surprise, but I definitely got more than I bargained for with Diego.

"Are you trying to get me the sack?" he asks in his seductive, Spanish accent.

"No, I'm trying to get you *in* the sack." I manage to mumble as our lips hurriedly crash together.

This is how it is with Diego; hot, urgent and passionate. *All the time.*

"What does that mean? Is that an English phrase?" he asks as he tangles his fingers in my hair and pulls me even closer.

"It means you and I need to be naked. Now."

He groans a deep, throaty moan and nips at my neck.

"You know I'm working. If the boss catches me doing this in here, he'll castrate me. I'll come to your room later," he promises, running his nose and lips up and down my neck.

"Ok." I pout. "But when?"

"I finish at four today. I'll come for you straight away."

"Not that fast I hope."

Diego looks utterly confused by my joke. Humour often seems to get lost in translation between us. *Just as well we hardly spend any time talking.*

"Later then." I kiss him hard once more and make sure I press right up against him and absorb as much of him as I can to last me until later. He's more addictive than any drug.

I turn and leave Diego standing in the spa, breathless, making sure I put some extra sway in my hips as I walk away. I know he's watching me leave.

When I return to my friends, they're all laying round the pool in bikinis, sipping Margaritas.

"Hey girl, how's lover boy?" Aimee asks, lowering her shades to look at me.

"Absolutely gorgeous," I reply with a dreamy smile.

The others roll their eyes and go back to their magazines or sunbathing. *I think they're sick of hearing about Diego.* Aimee is the die-hard romantic in the group, so she laps this shit up like its warm milk.

"Whatever you do, Olivia, DO NOT fall for this guy," Lauren says. "You have to leave him in eleven days so you can't afford to get attached."

"I know, I won't." I lie through my teeth. *Too late, I think I've already fallen hook, line and sinker.*

I already know what they think of him. They don't need to say it. They think he's just using me for a good time while I'm here and that I'm just one of many for Diego. *I don't believe that.* It's not worth arguing with them about it though. They've always been negative and opinionated, especially when it comes to me. I don't even know why they invite me places.

Eventually four o'clock comes and I'm ready and waiting in my room. I've asked the girls to make themselves scarce. They were only too happy to oblige. Lauren says we make her want to vomit.

Just as I finish brushing my wavy, black hair, I hear a knock at the door. I hurry over, in my lacy lingerie, to open it. Diego is standing there with a powder blue shirt on, unbuttoned half-way down, and a pair of black jean shorts. His sunglasses are perched on top of his head, nestled in his mass of dark curls.

"Hola Señorita," he says sexily. Diego speaks perfect English, but he knows it drives me wild when he speaks in Spanish.

"Hola yourself."

He looks me up and down like a hungry lion before kicking the door closed and pouncing on his prey. His lips instantly find mine as he grabs my hips and hoists me up so my legs wrap round his waist. Carrying me to the table with his hands fisted in my hair, he tugs gently so my head tips back and he can kiss my throat. He lowers me on to the table and I hurriedly start to unbutton the rest of his shirt. When I reach round to unclip my bra, he stops me.

"No, leave it on," he murmurs. "I like this outfit."

We're in such a lust-filled frenzy that his clothes are on my floor within seconds of him arriving. He tries to move me further up the table, but I lose my grip with the speed of the maneuver. My arm shoots out to steady myself, knocking two glasses and a bowl off the edge, causing them to crash to the floor in a shattered mess.

"Oops!" I giggle.

Diego laughs but doesn't lose focus. We both have one goal in mind, and we won't stop until we get there. He pulls my underwear to one side, allowing him access to where he craves. There's no need for foreplay between us, we've both been waiting for this all day. In no time at all, he's rolled a condom on and is ready to go. Diego grabs hold of my hips and pulls me towards him as he thrusts inside me, hard and fast. I cry out in pleasure as he pulls my arms above my head, sending more glasses and crockery crashing to the floor. He sets a punishing rhythm right from the start. Sex with Diego is the most intense thing I've ever experienced. He's so passionate, neither of us can seem to get enough of each other. He pounds into me, over and over again, as we both chase our orgasm.

The table creaks beneath us and vibrates across the floor from the force. More crockery and cutlery fall off the edge. Diego moans, a deep guttural sound, and widens his stance so he can increase the delicious friction between us further. I grip the table's edge in an attempt to hold on to reality as my pleasure spirals out of control. Diego slams into me harder and harder. Just when I think I can't take any more, we tip over the edge into ecstasy and he roars through our climax. With the final, brutal thrust, the table gives way beneath us with an almighty crack and we both fall to the floor along with the pieces of broken table and remaining glassware.

We both lay there, shocked and breathless for a moment, before bursting into laughter.

"Are you hurt?" he asks breathlessly.

"Not really, I think I bruised my elbow," I say, reaching round to have a look.

"Maybe we should have used the bed," Diego comments, looking round at the carnage we've caused.

He helps pull me up so we can assess how bad it is. *It's bad.*

"The girls are going to kill me for losing the security deposit."

"Don't worry about that, I'll sort it out." He flashes me a handsome smile as he pulls his shorts back on.

Just as I wrap myself in one of the fluffy hotel robes, there's a knock at the door. I'm not expecting anyone, and the girls all have key cards.

"Hello?" I open the door to find a tall, broad man in a black security t-shirt on the other side.

"Hello Miss, a disturbance was reported from this room. Someone said they could hear smashing and screaming. Are you ok?" His expression is deadly serious, only making this even funnier.

I snigger and rake my fingers through my wild, 'just fucked' hair. "Yes, thank you, I'm absolutely fine." I can't help it, but I start to laugh.

Opening the door a little wider, I call to Diego, "Apparently, we disturbed the other guests. Security is here."

Diego comes rushing to the door, still shirtless. His sun-kissed six pack on display for all to see.

"Diego?" the guy in the security shirt looks shocked to see him.

"Stan, listen, sorry for the disturbance. We will get this cleaned up right away and paid for."

"Diego, what are you doing in here with a guest?" His eyes scan the wrecked room behind me, then flit between a barely dressed Diego and me in a robe. Realisation dawns on his face and his features become even more stern.

"Stan, please. We didn't mean to break stuff. I'll take care of it." Diego pleads.

"You know the boss has strict rules on relations with guests. If he finds out about this, you'll be fired. You know that, right?" Stan folds his massive arms across his chest.

"I know. I'm sorry to put you in this position. Please keep quiet just this once, it won't happen again."

Stan huffs and cricks his neck. "Just this once. Get this shit cleaned up. You owe me Diego, big time."

After he leaves, I glare at Diego. "Won't happen again, huh?" *Nothing stings like a harsh slap in the face from reality.*

"I didn't mean *us,* I just meant, you know, not in the hotel or breaking stuff."

"Well, that's not what it sounded like, Diego. This is just a casual holiday hook-up to you, isn't it?" My friends' comments from earlier are ringing in my ears, causing my paranoid brain to go into overdrive. *Maybe they're right.*

"Olivia, I…" Unfortunately for Diego, he pauses a second longer than necessary, sending my insecurities and temper spiralling.

"Just go, Diego. Get out!" I yell, throwing his shirt and shoes at him. *Some holiday romance this is turning out to be.*

Claire

OCEAN'S APART

AT SOME POINT I must have fallen asleep after my row with Tony. When I wake up, the morning sun is streaming through the window. Hundreds of tiny rainbows dance round the room from a vase on the windowsill. I didn't realise how tired I was. I haven't slept that well for ages. Sitting up, I notice that Tony never came to bed as his side is totally undisturbed. *Where has he been?* A sickening feeling settles in the pit of my stomach as I wonder if he went back to the woman downstairs.

I find him asleep on the sofa and relief washes over me. My initial reaction is to feel guilty that he slept on the sofa all night but then I realise it's so luxurious, I imagine it's comfier than our bed at home, anyway.

Not wanting to disturb him, I dress and grab some swimming essentials. I leave him a note to say where I am and that I appreciate the thinking space. As I sling my beach bag over my shoulder and re-tie my sarong, I take one last look at my sleeping husband. *I really wish things weren't this difficult.* Sometimes I look at him like right now and I can't remember a single reason why I get so mad at him. Other times I want to wring his neck with my bare hands. *Surely that's not how marriage is supposed to be?*

When I get to the pool, I grab myself a sun bed and order a piña colada. *Nothing says 'summer holiday' like a piña colada!* It's still only mid-morning, but what the hell! The pool area is fairly quiet with just a handful of people in and around the water. It's nice to just sit in the sun and people watch for a while. Watching other people, though, I can't help but wonder what goes on in their relationships. *Are they as happy as they look or is it all for show? Who can say?*

My thoughts are interrupted by an elderly lady who shuffles up to the sun bed next to mine.

"Mind if I sit here, dear?" Despite her frailty and obvious difficulties with mobility, she clearly takes pride in her appearance and is maintaining the glamour of her youth with sophisticated dignity.

"Not at all," I say, gesturing to the empty seat.

"You look like you have the weight of the world on your shoulders, dear. Care to share?" The woman gives me a warm smile and slowly perches on the edge of her sunbed.

"Oh, I'm fine, really. Thank you, though," I say politely.

"I know that look. That is a 'man trouble' look." She looks at me with a mischievous twinkle in her eye. *I like this lady already.*

"You don't live to my age, dear, without learning a thing or two about man troubles. Come on, let's hear it and see what we can do. A problem shared is a problem halved and all that."

To my total surprise, whilst waiting for my response, this sweet little old lady in front of me beckons the waiter over and orders herself a cocktail to match mine!

"I'm here with my husband," I start to explain. I don't know what it is about this lady that makes me want to spill my guts to her. "It's kind of a last chance to save our marriage type situation," I say sadly.

She nods thoughtfully. "What went wrong?"

"I'm not even really sure anymore." I admit. "We just lost ourselves along the way, I think. We both work too much. We don't prioritise each other and we tried for several years to have children but failed. All those things take their toll, I guess. Now here we are." It actually felt surprisingly good to say all of that out loud.

The lady leans forward and squeezes my hand. Her skin is so soft, like velveteen. She smiles at me warmly and her kind face crinkles round her eyes and lips.

"Any words of wisdom?" I ask hopefully.

"I've been married a really long time dear, and do you know what I've learned in all those years?"

I shake my head.

"To let it go," she answers softly.

"Let what go?" I ask her as the waiter puts down the cocktail in front of her.

"All of it. The hurt, the anger, the pain, you have to let it all go." She lets go of my hand so she can take a sip of her drink, giving me time to think about what she just said.

Before I have a chance to respond, she continues, "If you don't, you will wake up one day and realise you let a good thing slip through your fingers."

This intriguing little lady in front of me talks a lot of sense. She's so wise and knowledgeable and yet even at her age, she hasn't let the world taint her and make her cynical. *I could learn a lot from this woman.*

"I think you could be right but I'm afraid it might already be too late." As I say the words out loud, I realise that I genuinely mean them.

"It's never too late, dear. It isn't over, until it's over." She gives me a cheeky wink and sips her cocktail. "If you love each other, you will find a way."

Five minutes with this remarkable lady has me feeling better than I've felt in months. *Maybe she's right. Maybe we can do this.*

"Anyway, enough about me. What brings you to The Paradise Hotel?" I ask her, genuinely wanting to know more about her.

"Well, this is my son, Alex's hotel and my husband has brought me here for our golden wedding anniversary." I can tell just from her facial expression as she talks about them, how much her family means to her.

"Oh congratulations! How lovely!" I start to say.

"He's dying; my husband," she interrupts. "He has a rare form of cancer and doesn't have long. The silly old fool thinks I don't know and that he's managed to keep it from me."

"Oh, my goodness, I'm so very sorry." I've only just met this lady, but my heart is breaking for her.

"Whatever for, dear?" she asks, looking genuinely bewildered.

"I'm so sorry to hear about your husband." I say quietly, trying to hold back the tears that are threatening and a little confused by her question.

"Don't be. That's just the way of things. Everybody dies eventually and Frank has done everything he wanted to in his life. We've had a ball. The funny thing is that he thinks after all these years he can keep something like that from me. In all the years I've known him, he has never once successfully kept a secret." She gets the most faraway look in her eyes as if she's remembering a different time.

"You're so brave. How do you hold it all together like that?" I ask her, feeling ridiculous that I seem more emotional than her right now.

"I let it go," she says with a sad smile. "I can either be sad and angry that I'm going to lose him and waste what time we have left wallowing, or I can choose to let it go and enjoy the time we have left. I choose the latter."

This lady is absolutely amazing. She puts me to shame. If she can be so brave and positive about something so heart-breaking, then surely, I can put the effort in to save my marriage?

A single tear escapes, despite my best efforts, and slides down my cheek.

"You're such a lovely lady," I whisper through my silent tears. "I'm so glad to have met you."

She takes both my hands in hers again and squeezes tight. "Everything happens for a reason, dear."

The spell of our heartfelt moment is broken by a member of staff.

"I'm so sorry to interrupt you Margaret, but Alex is asking for you. He says it's urgent."

Margaret, as I now know her, nods her head and starts to stand, using the young barman as a support to help her up.

"Thank you," she says to him before turning back to me. "Good luck dear. Everything will turn out just the ways it's supposed to. You'll see."

Just as quickly as my encounter with Margaret started, it ended. As I watch her leave, trying to wrap my head around her story and all the things she just said, I can't shake the feeling that my meeting with her was meant to be. I've never really believed in guardian angels, but somehow, I think I may have just met mine.

Margaret

SUNSET

"WHERE'S THE FIRE, SON?" I ask Alex when I eventually reach his office. It's incredibly frustrating now that my body can no longer keep up with my mind. It's just taken me the best part of ten minutes to walk here from my sun-lounger. "I was having a very nice chat with a lovely lady downstairs which you've dragged me away from."

I take a seat in his office to get my breath back and help myself to a lemon bon-bon from the bowl on his desk.

"I apologise," he says, kissing me on the cheek. "I want to talk to you about Dad."

I stiffen in my chair. *I knew this was coming. Alex is a smart man; he was going to figure it out some time. Only problem is, it shouldn't come from me.*

"Have you noticed him acting... odd lately?" He stops what he's doing and looks at me, concerned.

"Odd how, dear?" I feign ignorance.

"I don't know, I can't quite put my finger on it but he keeps fussing about his affairs and money which isn't like him and he keeps asking me if I remember different things from my childhood."

I shrug, trying to act casual. "Oh, you know your father, Alex. He's always been a quirky old coot."

I don't want to mislead Alex, but he needs to hear this from Frank. *Hell, it'd be nice if I heard this from Frank.*

"You would tell me if there was something wrong with Dad, wouldn't you?" Alex's eyes are filled with concern.

"If you're worried then go talk to him about it. Nothing good ever came of bottling things up."

I give him a warm smile and pat the back of his hand across the desk, satisfied that I've deflected hi question without lying to him, for now.

"Now if you don't mind, I'd like to go back to soaking up some sun and sipping cocktails."

Alex chuckles and helps me out of the chair. "Just don't go causing any trouble. This is a respectable resort."

"As if I would." I give my son a cheeky wink and shuffle out of his office.

I'm so very proud of that boy. He's really made something of himself here. I can't say I was overly happy when he first moved to Spain but having watched him turn this place into the wonder it is now and seeing how happy it makes him, how could I not be pleased for him? If he could just find a nice girl to marry, then my life's work will be complete.

I decide instead of going back to the pool that it's high time I had a chat with Frank. I've gone along with this charade of him not being ill for long enough. I know he will have his reasons for trying to hide it from us, but we have always faced things together and this should be no different. *Especially this.*

"Hello darling," I greet him when I get back to our room. He's sitting in a big armchair reading the newspaper.

Frank lowers the newspaper and looks at me over his reading glasses. "You look nice."

"Thank you," I smile and fluff my short, permed hair with my palm. "So, what's happening in the world today?" I ask him, taking a seat in the chair next to his. We sit the exact same way at home, side by side in two matching armchairs like a pair of bookends.

"Not much, the stock market has dipped again and we lost the rugby," he says gruffly, folding the newspaper and putting it on the coffee table.

"That hardly counts as news," I reply. "Did you remember to make our table reservation for tonight?"

"Yes dear," he mumbles sarcastically. "As if you'd let me forget."

Frank takes his glasses off and starts to clean them on the edge of his beige, flannel shirt. Even at our age, after all this time, I still think he's the most handsome man in the room, wherever we go.

"Frank?" I ask softly.

He puts his glasses back on and smiles at me warmly, through clean, shiny lenses.

"Are you going to tell me why we're here?"

He gives me a puzzled look. "You know why we're here. It's our golden anniversary. Fifty years of marriage is something worth celebrating, don't you think?"

"I quite agree, but you and I both know that's not the real reason you brought me here." I give him a heartfelt look. *As much as I meant what I said to the lovely young lady downstairs, this is still a difficult conversation to have.*

"I don't understand." Frank says quietly, turning in his chair so he's facing me.

"I know about the cancer, Frank," I say gently, reaching across and placing my hand on top of his. He always used to hold my hand whenever he took me on a date. It was one of the many things that made me fall for him.

Frank's face falls and he drops his eyes, unable to look at me. "How do you know?" he murmurs.

"Darling, you're not as sneaky as you think you are. I suspected for a while and then I found one of your hospital letters." I squeeze his hand that little bit tighter.

My husband may be dying but I will never truly let him go.

He nods in acknowledgement, still looking at his trouser leg. "I'm so sorry Maggie. I didn't want to worry you. I thought..."

"You thought if you buried your head in the sand then it would go away?"

"Yeah, something like that." His voice starts to wobble but he fights to keep it together.

"Look at me, Frank."

Slowly he takes a deep breath and raises his eyes to look at me. Even though his eyes are sad and tired now, they are still beautiful to me.

"Whatever happens, and whatever you want to do, I'm here. We do it together, just like we've always done. Did you honestly think after all the storms we've weathered together in our life that I wouldn't stand shoulder to shoulder with you for the final hurdle?" I ask calmly.

"No, I suppose you're right. You're a good woman, Maggie Andrews; the best." He pauses and continues to look into my eyes. "We had a good run, me and you." His lip starts to wobble and his voice cracks.

"We certainly did my darling, and it's not over yet. So, I say we stop moping up here and enjoy our last trip together. What do you think? One last hurrah?"

Franks smiles. "That sounds wonderful. What did you have in mind?"

"Dancing." I smile devilishly. It always was my favourite thing to do.

"Dancing it is." He ushers me over with his hand and taps his lap for me to come sit.

I slowly manage to get out of the chair and perch on his knee. Kissing the top of his forehead, I breathe in his familiar scent. He's washed with the same soap and shampoo for decades. There is no smell more homely and comforting than my Frank.

"You need to tell Alex, darling." I say gently as I smooth out his collar; an old habit.

"I know, I'll do it when the time is right. He will take good care of you, Maggie. He's a good boy."

"Oh, I know he will, he learned from the best." I plant a soft kiss on my husband's forehead and wonder how many more kisses we have left. I fear the sands of time are running out faster than I realised.

Alex

SHIPWRECKED

EVERY MORNING STARTS THE SAME; five o'clock wake up and have a freshly made smoothie before my run along the beach. I like to get out and exercise, clear my head before the hotel starts to wake and the day starts. I've had the same routine for years.

This morning is no different, I've just downed a glass of freshly squeezed pineapple and coconut with a whole bunch of other disgustingly healthy ingredients thrown in for good measure. I grab my phone in case someone needs me inside and begin my jog along the deserted beach. I love this time of the morning, it's so quiet and peaceful. It's just me and the ocean. This morning there is a particularly stunning sunrise, sparkling on the waves, and a cool, early morning breeze.

I look across the endless horizon as I jog through the surf thinking about the things I need to get done today. Thoughts of my dad keep popping into my head and I make a mental note to make sure I find time to talk to him today.

I've been running about ten minutes when I notice something floating in the surf, further down the beach. The closer I get, the sicker I feel as it dawns on me that this may not be a something, but a someone. *Shit.* I pick up the pace and sprint the rest of the way to what I can now tell is a woman bobbing face down in the shallow water. Her hair splayed out across the waves like a golden fan. *Double shit! What the hell happened? I don't do drama and scandal at my resort.* I need to fix this and fast before anyone else sees her. I have no idea whether she's dead or alive.

As I start to wade through the water towards her, I take my phone out of my pocket and call Jackson. He's my second in command and will be able to help me take care of this situation. *Whatever it is.*

"Jackson, meet me at the beach. We have a situation," I tell him hurriedly.

"Be there in five, boss." I hang up the phone and tuck it back in my shorts pocket.

The water is only knee deep when I get closer to her. Placing my arms under her chest I gently scoop her and roll her over on my arms so I can see her face. I let out a breath I hadn't realised I was holding when I see that she still has a little bit of colour to her cheeks. *Thank God, I think she's still alive.*

I carry her out of the water and place her gently in the

sand so I can check for a pulse. Just as I find one Jackson comes sprinting across the sand.

"What the hell happened here?" he asks, panting as he stops next to us. "Is she alive?"

"Barely. I've found a weak pulse but she's not breathing. Call an ambulance while I start CPR," I instruct.

I begin chest compressions on her limp form. She looks like she's in her twenties but it's hard to tell. If it weren't for the deathly blue tinge round her lips and the dark circles under her eyes, she would be considered beautiful. *God only knows how long she's been in the water for.* She wobbles lifelessly under the force of my compressions and sinks a little into the wet sand under my weight. After thirty brutal compressions, I stop and tip her head back slightly, giving her two rescue breaths. Nothing.

I can hear Jackson speaking to the emergency services as I go back to counting to thirty once more. I need to be firm for this to work but she seems so fragile under my hands. I'm scared of breaking a rib. *Better that than dying. Come on, breathe!* I try to will her back to life. Whoever this woman is, she doesn't deserve to die on my beach.

After five punishing rounds of chest compressions and mouth to mouth, I'm just about to ask Jackson to swap with me as I'm starting to tire when she suddenly splutters to life beneath me. She starts to cough up water, so I roll her onto her side while it all comes up. Once she's finished spewing up sea water her chest heaves as she dry retches. Her body desperately trying to drag oxygen into her lungs.

"It's ok, you're alright." I try to soothe her by stroking her hair and speaking gently. Her eyes are wild and frantic with panic. Despite the severity of the situation, the incredible colour of her eyes doesn't escape my attention. I've never seen a colour quite like it. A flecked mix of greens and blues, seemingly always changing.

The mysterious woman with the unusual eyes tries to sit up as she continues to cough. I put my hand on her shoulder to steady her. Her whole body is shaking, probably from the cold and shock. It's a toasty twenty-eight degrees already this morning but I imagine being in the water for what appears to have been some time has drastically reduced her body temperature.

"Jackson, can you get someone to send blankets down to keep her warm, then go and meet the ambulance so they know where to find us?"

"Yep, on it." Jackson sprints back up the beach towards the hotel leaving me alone with this poor, fragile creature.

"It's ok, you're alright." I repeat gently as I rub in circular motions on her back to calm her down and warm her.

Gradually she starts to calm and her breathing slows down a little as the coughing subsides.

"There's an ambulance on its way, sweetheart. What's your name?"

"Sienna" she croaks. Her throat is so hoarse from all the water, and I can tell by her face how painful it is to speak.

I don't ask her anymore questions. I just continue to talk to her and comfort her until eventually Jackson appears with two paramedics and an armful of blankets.

I quickly wrap the blankets around Sienna's shoulders as I explain to the paramedics what little I know. Handing her over to their care, I gesture to Jackson for him to step aside so I can talk to him in private.

"I don't want a word of this to get out. Especially not until we know what happened to her. Get this part of the beach screened off until the emergency services are finished. It's still early so not many people will be up yet. I need to head back up to the hotel but keep me updated as to how she's doing."

Jackson nods. "You got it, boss."

I walk back over to where Sienna is sat huddled in her pile of blankets next to the paramedics as they check her over and ask her questions.

"I have to go to work now, so I will leave you with the paramedics who will take good care of you. This is Jackson, he is here to help too. Anything you need, just ask. My name's Alex by the way," I explain as I'm crouched in front of her. I take one last look at those beautiful eyes before I stand and turn.

"Alex?" she croaks.

"Yes?" I say as I turn back towards her.

"Thank you," she says with shy embarrassment which is a vast improvement on unconscious.

I nod at her and smile. "You're welcome, Sienna. Take care of yourself."

With that I jog back to the hotel to start my day. Knowing more than likely Sienna will be taken to hospital and I will never see her again or find out her story. *Life's weird that way.*

As I approach the main doors, I can see my mother standing in the doorway watching the events unfold. *I might have known she'd be awake and watching. Nothing gets past that woman.*

"Mother." I greet her with a nod and a kiss on her crinkled cheek.

"It's a little early to be giving mermaids the kiss of life, son," she says with a smile.

I chuckle. My mother has always had a vivid imagination.

"She's not a mermaid. She's a very lucky young lady."

"That she is, my boy. She met you, didn't she?"

I roll my eyes at my mother's meddling riddles. I have no clue what she's talking about half the time, but she means well.

"Yes well, she'll be off to hospital now and so I imagine that's the end of that." I shrug.

"Don't be so sure, Alex. I think you'll be seeing a lot more of that little mermaid. You mark my words," she says, winking and giving my arm a squeeze.

I highly doubt it but a small part of me wonders, maybe even hopes that my mother is right. She's always had an uncanny ability to predict the future. *Time will tell I suppose.*

ONCE THE DAY GETS GOING, it is a busy one as always. Paradise isn't as relaxing as it looks when you're the one running it. Just before lunch, Jackson comes to find me in my office.

"Hey Alex, thought I'd update you on this morning's mystery woman," he says, coming in and taking a seat.

"Hmm, yes. How is she doing?"

"Well, she left with the paramedics for a check-up. They're confident that she's doing ok but want to be sure. Before they left though I did find out that she's a guest here at the hotel and she's on her honeymoon."

A mixture of anger and disappointment overwhelms me. Anger, that whoever she's married to, didn't take better care of her and disappointment that she's even married at all.

"Well, where the hell is her damn husband?" I ask, not really expecting an answer. I tap my pen on my desk while I think. "Find him. Look up his room number and find him. We need to speak to this arsehole and find out why he wasn't anywhere to be seen while his new bride was floating face down in the ocean." *Why am I so angry about this? I don't even know this woman.*

All day I've been telling myself it's because I don't want the hassle and the drama of a scandal but it's more than that. The mysterious 'mermaid,' as my mother refers to her, with the hypnotic eyes has got under my skin. Without even realising it, Sienna is rapidly seeping into my system like the ink of a fresh tattoo.

"Or..." says Jackson tentatively. "Counter proposal. We don't go steaming in there like a band of thugs without knowing the facts. The paramedics were confident Sienna would be released again later today or tomorrow so why don't we wait for her to return and find out what happened first?"

This is why Jackson and I work so well together; I think with my heart, he thinks with his head.

"Ok, you might be right. Would you phone the hospital please and find out her release details? Pretend to be her husband if you have to. Then reserve her the best suite we have available so she can rest and recover."

Jackson nods. "Great idea, boss." He smiles a knowing smile before turning to leave.

"Oh, and Jackson?" I call. "Find out who her husband is and have security keep a close eye on him until we know more."

It seems my mother might have been right after all.

Sienna

SHIPWRECKED

WHAT A COMPLETE AND UTTER DISASTER. How can things have gone so badly wrong, so fast? This is supposed to be my honeymoon, but instead it's turned into a living nightmare.

I arrive back at The Paradise Hotel after being discharged from the hospital. I don't fully understand what happened, but from the bits of broken English and Spanish I picked up, it seems someone from the hotel arranged my travel back here. It won't have been my *husband*; I don't think he even knows what happened. *Maybe it was the man who saved me?*

I'm greeted at the hotel doors by the other man who'd come to my rescue this morning. *I think he said his name was Jackson?* So much has happened, some of the details are a little fuzzy.

"Hello, Sienna. How are you feeling?" he asks politely. Unlike this morning he is dressed in a dinner suit now with a black bow tie.

"Much better, thank you," I say shyly with embarrassment. I still sound awful when I speak. My throat feels like I've swallowed barbed wire.

"Alex has upgraded you to the best suite available so you can recover and rest. I'll show you to your new room but if you need anything at all, please just ask."

I feel so confused. *Who is Alex?* So much has happened to me since the wedding. I'm having trouble keeping up. My thoughts and emotions feel torn up and scattered like confetti. The confusion on my face must be obvious because Jackson adds, "Alex owns the hotel. He's the one who pulled you out of the water. He's incredibly worried about you and wants to make sure you're properly looked after."

Alex, that's right. Yes, I do remember his name now. He was like a beacon of calm this morning in my own personal hell. *I need to find him and thank him.* Not only did he save my life today but now he's being more generous than I could ever imagine.

Jackson shows me to my new room which is on the other side of the hotel to my first room. I must admit I'm rather relieved, avoiding Mason is my number one priority right now.

When we step through into the new room, it's incredible. I thought our previous room was luxurious, but this is something else entirely. There is an enormous four poster bed with white linen curtains and a spa bath that's the size of a small pool. A huge platter of fresh fruits and pastries has been laid out on the side for me and there is a bottle of champagne on ice.

"Oh my goodness, this is too much!" I exclaim in shock.

"It's what Alex wants you to have. Get some rest, it's been a long day."

Looking around, I realise that all my stuff is already here. *When did it all get moved over? What does Mason think of all this?* So many questions.

"Thank you so much, for everything," I say, still looking around in disbelief. I hesitate before saying, "Can I ask you something?"

"Of course."

"Where is Mason, my... husband?" I almost choke on the word as bile fills my throat. "Does he know where I am?"

"No need to worry, Sienna. Alex has taken care of everything."

What does that even mean? As if he can read my mind, he adds, "Alex will be along later to check on you. You can ask him everything yourself then."

Jackson smiles at me warmly before leaving me alone. This is the first time I've been alone all day and suddenly the enormity of everything that's happened hits me like a tidal wave. I flop on the enormous bed and start to sob. Loud, ugly, chest-heaving sobs. Even though my chest and throat still hurt like hell from all the water I took in, I can't stop crying.

I think eventually I must've cried myself to sleep because I'm woken by a gentle knocking on the door. *Oh God I must look like shit!* I stop at the floor to ceiling mirror by the door and try to smooth my hair down and pinch some colour into my cheeks. Thankfully it's not too obvious I've been crying; the puffy red eyes are hardly noticeable now I've slept.

"Hello?" I call through the door.

"Sienna, it's Alex. I was just coming to check you're alright." His voice is so soothing, it almost wafts under the door like smoke and envelopes me in a cocoon of calm.

I open the door slowly to face the man who brought me back to life.

"Hi Alex," I say quietly, trying to disguise just how awful my voice still sounds. "I don't know how to ever thank..." I start, but he cuts me off.

"Think nothing of it. May I come in?" He looks past me into the room as if checking no one else is there.

"Of course." I step aside as he walks briskly into the room, leaving an intoxicating aroma of aftershave in his wake. Just like Jackson, he too is now dressed in a dinner suit with a bow tie. He takes a seat on the enormous corner sofa and gestures for me to sit with him. *How can someone be so calming and dominant all at the same time?*

"How are you feeling?" he asks. His eyes roam all over my face and body. Not in an uncomfortable way, more in a check-up sort of way as if looking for obvious signs of injury.

"Much better than I was, thank you." I tuck my hair behind my ears, nervously. *Why does this man have me so confused?*

"Tell me what happened to you Sienna, please?" He looks at me intensely and for some unknown reason I feel compelled to tell him my story. You'd think the events of the past few days would have taught me not to trust so easily but there's something about this man that puts me at ease.

"It was an accident. I wasn't trying to drown myself."

His eyes never leave mine. "Well, I'm pleased to hear that."

I find myself watching the shape of his lips as he speaks. *What the hell is wrong with me? I'm in the middle of this monumental fuck up and here I am day-dreaming over a total stranger's lips.*

"So how did you come to end up floating face down on my shore?" I don't know whether it's intentional or not but I'm sure each time he speaks he gets a little closer. "I thought you were dead."

"I'm so sorry you had to find me like that, but I'm so grateful that you did. You're the reason I'm alive." Without realising it, I've started to lean closer too, gravitating towards him like a magnet.

He clears his throat and loosens his bow tie, breaking eye contact for the first time since we sat down. There's no denying the raw sexual tension in the room. I continue with my story before he has a chance to speak.

"I got married three days ago to a man I barely know. It was *good for business,*" I say, imitating my father's tone of voice. "My father is not someone you argue with, so after meeting Mason a few times I reluctantly agreed. He seemed nice enough. We went out a few times and he was very polite and respectful. Our families arranged the wedding and neither of us had much say in the plans." I'm painfully aware of how ridiculous my life sounds now that I'm hearing it out loud. "The wedding was an over-the-top showcase of wealth. I hardly recognised anyone there. It was just an elaborate networking stunt really."

Alex has gone back to watching me intently. I've never had a man give me such undivided attention before.

"Once the wedding was over, we flew straight here for our honeymoon courtesy of his parents. That's when things started to really unravel." I fidget on the sofa knowing the next part of the story is hard to say.

"Mason made it clear he had certain *expectations*, what with it being our wedding night and our honeymoon. I told him I needed time and wanted to get to know him better first." Dropping my eyes to my lap I tuck more stray strands of hair behind my ears.

"Sienna, what did he do to you?" When I look up, Alex's aura of calm has been replaced with fire and anger. His eyes are blazing.

"He tried to force himself on me and when I refused, he grabbed me by the throat and threw me at the wall." My scratchy voice cracks at the end as I give in to the fear and upset I've been bottling up for the past few days.

Alex's jaw tenses as he tries to keep his mask of calm in place but it's slipping. The more I tell him the more tense he gets. His anger doesn't scare me though, I'm actually touched that this man who knows nothing about me cares enough to feel something about my story.

"Go on." he says gently.

I take a deep breath before continuing. "I left and made myself scarce for the rest of the evening trying to figure out what I should do. I tried calling my parents, they wouldn't hear of it. My mother's exact words were 'you need to give it time darling'. As if what happened is perfectly normal! Eventually I ran out of things to do so I went back to the room only to discover Mason was in there with someone else. *Balls deep* in someone else to be exact. He didn't even have the decency to stop fucking her. He just smirked at me and said, 'Well if you won't give me what I want sweetheart, I'll get it somewhere else' as he carried on."

Alex bangs his fists on the glass coffee table making me jump. "Fucking low-life piece of shit!" he growls, almost under his breath.

"Sorry Sienna, I didn't mean to startle you. I just can't even begin to understand how he could treat you like that."

I give a small smile and a shrug. *Neither do I.*

"Anyway, what happened next was entirely my fault and a complete accident. I ran from the room humiliated and went straight to the bar to buy a bottle of tequila. I'm not usually much of a drinker, hence why that plan didn't work out so well. Over the next few hours, I drank most of the bottle and cried, *a lot.* I was sitting on the beach, wallowing in what a nightmare my life had become, and I just wanted to drift away. I was never trying to kill myself; I just didn't want to be *me* anymore. I waded out into the water in the darkness and just floated, looking up at the stars."

I pause letting the reality of all what's happened to me sink in. It's the first time I've explained it all. At the hospital I only outlined the basics the best I could in a mix of terrible Spanish and English.

"The next thing I remember is waking up on the beach with you."

I meet Alex's gaze again for the first time since starting my story. I can't tell at all what he's thinking. He just continues to look at me without saying a word.

"Please say something," I whisper.

"I'm so very sorry, Sienna. I promise that from now on, while you're under this roof, you are safe." He looks at me with such sincerity that I actually believe that he means it.

"I'll take care of Mason," he adds sternly.

"No, Alex. I don't want any trouble. This is my mess. Let me handle this."

For the first time since entering the room, Alex actually touches me. He picks up my hand and holds it in his. A warm feeling starts at my hand and spreads all over my body.

"You almost died. All you need to worry about is feeling better. Why don't you get some rest and we can talk about this more tomorrow?"

I nod and smile appreciatively. "Thank you."

"Think nothing of it, my little mermaid." he says quietly.

Raising one eyebrow, I give him a quizzical look, not understanding the reference.

"My mother's nickname for you. She saw me pull you out of the water."

"I like that." I laugh, but it hurts. My chest is still painful from the CPR.

"Get some rest," Alex says as he stands and heads to the door. "I'll see you in the morning."

With that, my handsome rescuer leaves me alone with my thoughts and demons. *What the hell do I do now?*

Alex

SHIPWRECKED

AFTER LEAVING Sienna's room I go straight to find Mason. Flanked by Stan and Marco, two of the best men on my security team, I knock on the door.

When the door opens, we're greeted by a man not very big in stature, wearing a Hawaiian style shirt and shorts. His dirty blonde, floppy hair is swept back off his face with some sort of overly shiny styling product.

"Mason Hargreaves?" I ask, deliberately keeping my face serene.

"Who's asking?" he replies rudely as he drains the remainder of the champagne he's holding and discards the glass on the side table.

"My name's Alex Andrews. That's a name you're going to want to remember. I'm the owner of this establishment."

Mason eyes Marco and Stan suspiciously. They are both easily twice his size in build, as am I and probably almost a foot taller. They look pretty menacing with their black t-shirts stretched round their bulging biceps.

"Well, good for you. Nice place you have here. What can I do for you fellas?" The words might be polite, but his tone is not. He folds his arms across his chest trying to appear bigger than he is.

"You can get out of my hotel...now," I say calmly.

"I beg your pardon? I'm a paying customer and this place was not cheap! I think you need to work on your room service mate." He sneers.

Big mistake. I signal for Marco and Stan to enter his room with me to avoid a spectacle in the corridor. Mason's eyes widen in shock as he is forced to walk backwards allowing us inside. Stan closes the door quietly behind us.

"Hey, what do you think..." Mason starts to speak but he's cut off by Stan and Marco grabbing an arm each and holding him in place so I have his full attention.

"I suggest you listen carefully Mr Hargreaves because I shall say this only once. I do not allow, violent, wife beating thugs and adulterers into my hotel."

Mason opens his mouth to speak but I continue before he has the chance to speak. *It's my turn mother-fucker.*

"Are you aware that after you abused your wife on your wedding night and then humiliated her by inviting another woman into your bed, she ended up almost drowned on the beach after drinking a bottle of tequila?"

Mason smirks at me. "Not my fault the silly prude can't handle her drink."

This scumbag just signed his own death warrant. I grab his chin with one hand and get right in his face. He almost stumbles back in surprise but can't move because of Stan and Marco's vice-like grip.

"Does it make you feel big, picking on defenseless women? You low-life piece of shit. She was your wife! It was your wedding night!" I spit the words angrily at him.

"Some wedding night." He scoffs.

I'm gagging to pummel this prick's face in, but I know if I start, I won't stop until he's dead.

"Boys, please escort Mr Hargreaves off the premises and ensure that he stays that way. You have a lifetime ban here. If you ever try to enter my hotel again you will regret it." Narrowing my eyes and stepping back, I regain my composure somewhat.

"You can't do this! I'm going to sue your fucking arse!" He yells as he's marched down the corridor. "Where am I supposed to go?"

"You're a big man remember? You'll figure something out."

I follow behind them to the exit. Mason doesn't stand a chance of resisting them. They shove him out the door towards the drive and he stumbles on the bottom step.

"Make sure he's taken right off the property outside the gates. Oh and boys, rearrange his face before you leave him. He needs that sickening smirk wiping off it." I mutter in their ear.

Stan and Marco nod and usher Mason along the path. Satisfied that that's the last Sienna will see of him I turn and head back inside. When I get back to my office, I pour myself a stiff drink and slump in my chair. I'm just about to start shutting my computer down for the night when there's a knock at the door.

"Come in," I call before taking a sip and enjoying the burn of the whiskey on the way down.

Jackson steps into my office. "Long day huh?"

"Yea, you could say that." I undo my bow tie and lean back in my chair.

"Did you go visit Sienna? What did she say?" he asks folding his arms across his chest.

"Turns out her husband is a cheating, wife-beating scumbag. Needless to say, he's been removed." I throw back the rest of my whiskey and wince.

"Well good riddance. How's she's doing?"

"She's been through a lot but she's surprisingly well. That suite is hers for as long as she needs it."

"You got it boss. Anything else you need me to do before I go?" Jackson's a good man. He'd do anything for me and this hotel.

"No, you go. It's getting late. Thanks for everything today Jackson."

He nods his head once and gives an appreciative smile.

What a fucking day. Thankfully this high level of drama is rare around here. Somehow though I don't believe this week is done with me yet.

Olivia

INFERNO

THE LAST TWO days of the holiday have been almost unbearable. I haven't spoken to Diego out of stubbornness and spite since our fight the other night. I don't even really know why; I imagine the only person I'm really hurting is myself.

I made the stupid mistake of telling my friends what happened and they blew the whole thing way out of proportion in a way that only they can. They have made it their mission ever since to keep me as far away from Diego as possible and to distract me with other things. Needless to say, none of it has worked and I find myself thinking about him all the time.

I wonder whatever happened to the table? When I came back to the room there was a brand new one there as if nothing had ever happened. I haven't told the girls about that. I figured some things are best left unshared.

"Olivia, can you go and order us some more of those nachos and another round of drinks?" Lauren lowers her sunglasses as she talks to me from her ridiculously big pink lilo floating on the pool.

"Why me?" I snap back.

"Because you're the only one not in the pool." Lauren says matter-of-factly as she puts her sunglasses back in place and rests her head back on her inflatable monstrosity.

"Fine." I mutter under my breath as I stand up and grab my purse.

I decide to walk the long way round to the bar, past the entrance to the spa in hopes of bumping into Diego. I haven't even caught sight of him these past two days. *I'm starting to question my own sanity that I didn't make the whole thing up!*

My slow stroll past the spa doors is to no avail. No sign of Diego. I'm not sure it's normal to miss someone you've only just met. The longer he keeps his distance the more I wonder if my friends were right all along. Maybe I am just a holiday fling to him, possibly even one of many, *I mean look at him for Christ's sake, he's an exotic dream come true!*

I order the nachos and drinks and decide not to go the long way back. Maybe my story with Diego has run its course and was all it was ever supposed to be.

One thing I do know for sure is that I need to stop listening to my so-called friends. I met them in college and I used to be so shy and self-conscious back then. I think they liked having someone in the group they could boss around and manipulate to be honest. As the years have gone on though I have grown in confidence and started to see them for what they are.

I think part of the reason they discourage my relationship with Diego is out of jealousy. Who would've thought little Olivia would grow up to be hot enough to catch the eye of a man like Diego?

I take my place back on my sunbed and wait for the order to arrive. The others don't even notice I'm back. They're too busy gossiping in the pool like a gang of school girls. *Note to self, when I get home, it's time to get myself some new friends.*

Ignoring their childish antics, I try to go back to reading my book, but I just keep re-reading the same paragraph over and over again, not really taking any of it in. I can't stop thinking about Diego and whether there's a way to make things right between us before time runs out.

"Why don't you come join us?" Aimee asks from the edge of the water.

She's by far the nicest one of the group, if I had to pick just one of them to stay friends with, it would be Aimee.

"You know I don't like water." I reply without even looking up from my book.

"But it's so lovely and warm." Aimee argues.

"It's still wet though."

I've never liked water or anything to do with it ever since I was a child. I fell in a lake near my aunt's house when I was about seven years old and scared myself shitless. I've avoided all water and water-based activities ever since, I can swim. I just choose not to.

"Just leave her Aimee, you know she'll never get in for fear of having to strip off and someone realising she used to be fat." Lauren giggles from her lilo.

What I wouldn't give to push the silly cow off of it right now!

"Yes Lauren, we've all seen my childhood pictures, we all know I used to be the fat kid. At what point will this stop being funny to you?"

Never mind the fact that I've been a curvy size ten for the past eight years now, it will never be long enough for Lauren to forget that I used to be fat.

"You can't fat-shame people like that Lauren, it's the twenty first century." Aimee tries to stick up for me.

"I'm not fat-shaming anyone, am I Olivia? It was just a joke. Don't get your knickers in a twist."

I've heard just about enough of this idiocy. I need some space to think about more important things like how I'm going to fix things with Diego.

I get up from the sunbed and collect my book and bag before slipping away from the poolside. They haven't even noticed; they've gone back to whatever hot gossip has caught their attention now.

Walking back to our room I'm hit with a genius idea. *Maybe I'll book a massage with Diego so I can get him all to myself and apologise.* Recreating the exact same way we met might soften him up a little. *Although not everywhere I hope.*

I take my phone from my bag and dial the spa.

"Hello, yes. I'd like to book an appointment please."

Claire

OCEAN'S APART

SINCE MY CHAT with Margaret the other day, things have been much better between me and Tony. I barely slept that night thinking about what she said and I decided to take her advice. Tony and I had a lengthy discussion about our relationship, and I think it did us both good to air our views and vent our frustrations.

As part of our promise to each other to make amends and get back on track, Tony suggested we go to a salsa class the hotel is hosting on the beach tonight. When we were dating, he used to take me to a Mexican restaurant in the city that did salsa dancing in the evenings and we used to get drunk and dance the night away, *badly!*

I've been looking forward to it all day and I even bought myself a new dress in the boutique downstairs. It's a coral-coloured halter neck that fans out when I spin, showing a lot of leg and a plunging neck line. It's much bolder than anything I've worn for years but I figured we're on holiday and the whole idea is to have fun, so why not?! Plus, I want to make the effort and remind Tony what attracted us to each other in the first place.

"Wow, what a knockout!" Tony says when I emerge from the bathroom. He looks me up and down with a surprised grin on his face. "You look absolutely amazing, Claire."

I start smiling too, it feels nice to be noticed and complimented.

"Thank you." I plant a kiss on his cheek as I walk past him to get my shoes, taking him by surprise. *I can't actually remember the last time we showed each other any affection.*

I put my strappy heels on and pick up my matching clutch bag. "Ready?"

He looks so relaxed and happy; it's been a long time since I've seen him like this. He's wearing a cream short-sleeve shirt with his sunglasses hooked through his buttonhole and a pair of beige linen trousers. The pale colours are really highlighting his recently acquired tan. *How have I spent so many years not realising what's been right in front of me?*

Tony offers me his hand and I gladly accept. For the first time in a long time, we walk hand in hand through the hotel down to the beach. I haven't seen Tony's phone come out of his bag since we had our discussion. We're not out of the woods yet but I certainly feel more hopeful than ever that we stand a good chance of putting things right between us.

AN HOUR later and the salsa class is in full swing. A temporary dance floor has been put on the beach by the outside bar and lanterns hang in the palm trees. There really is no expense spared in this place. The instructor has spent time teaching us the basic steps and everyone is starting to relax and get the hang of it. I haven't had this much fun in years!

Tony is surprisingly good at this. *Who knew he could sway his hips like that?*

"Ok everybody, now you know the basic steps, we're going to try it with the music. Bailamos," says the instructor as he grabs an unsuspecting partner by the wrist.

Sensual salsa music fills the air and Tony takes me by the hand. He puts his other hand on my hip and pulls me close without warning. My pelvis collides with his and our noses touch as an unexpected electric-current runs through my entire body. I haven't felt anything like it for such a long time, *if ever.* After being with the same person for so long, I stopped expecting such a reaction. It feels as if something inside me is awakening after being dormant for longer than I care to admit.

Tony smiles confidently and whispers in my ear, "Ready?"

With his hand positioned on the small of my back, we grind and sway together to the rhythm of the music.

He's unbelievably good at this and leads me in the steps with ease. Suddenly he spins me round the dance floor really fast making me cry out in surprise and start laughing. My head is still spinning when he pulls me back close and goes back to grinding against me in time to the music.

"So where did this secret talent for salsa come from?" I shout over the music.

Tony smiles as he sends me into another spin. This time I lose my balance from the speed and bump into him with my hands on his chest.

"I don't know, just got an excellent partner I guess."

I can feel his heart beating fast from all the dancing. *Or maybe from the moment we seem to be having between us?* I realise I haven't stopped smiling the whole time we've been doing this and neither has he. I'm not sure whether my legs ache more or my face.

As we continue to dance, we look each other deep in the eyes, I mean *really* look at each other. Almost as if seeing each other for the first time. He has such a strong, handsome face, which obviously I knew, (we've been married eight years!) but I think I somehow *forgot.* Out of nowhere a rush of butterflies floods my stomach and I suddenly feel more nervous excitement than I did on our first date. I know he feels it too by the growing bulge in his trousers.

"Claire, I..." he starts to murmur in my ear when suddenly the music ends.

"Muy bien." The instructor announces. "You're all experts now, sí?" The instructor's unique blend of Spanish and English cuts through our moment.

Tony takes a step back and subtly tries to rearrange himself in his trousers, suddenly very aware that we are on a beach full of other people.

"Now we are going to change partners every time I shout switch." The instructor explains. "Chicos grab las chicas, ready? Uno, dos, tres, quattro!"

Before I even have time to realise what's happening, I'm spun away from Tony and claimed by a very enthusiastic man in a bright pink t-shirt.

"Hello," he says as he treads on my foot. What he lacks in dance skills, he more than makes up for with enthusiasm. "My name's Trent."

"Claire," I reply, distracted as I search the room for Tony and try to avoid being stepped on again.

Looking around the room I spot Margaret at the edge of the dance floor with whom I assume must be her husband. She looks ever so elegant in a long black sequined dress and they are swaying gently to the music together. She sees me too and gives me a little smile and wave.

I see Tony not too far away with a lady who looks like this evening is her worst nightmare. Tony is clearly trying to put her at ease but she couldn't look more bored if she tried. My partner on the other hand is still gyrating in front of me and dancing to what appears to be his own beat.

"Switch!" yells the instructor. *Thank goodness!*

I try to steer myself in Tony's direction but before I get there I'm swept in another direction by a pair of muscular arms.

"Hola, Claire isn't it?"

I look up at my new partner and realise it's the masseuse from the spa. I booked myself in there yesterday for a shoulder massage.

"Yes, hello again, Diego." I reply.

He really is a stunning looking man, and salsa dancing is clearly something that comes naturally to him. He isn't even concentrating as we talk.

"Are you having a nice evening?" he asks in between spins.

"Yes, thank you. It's great fun. Are you here with a partner?" I don't recall seeing him arrive.

"Not exactly. I am currently in, how do you say it? The dog's house?"

I giggle at his attempted translation. "Yes, oh dear. Well, I'm sure with moves like this she won't stay mad for long."

Diego twirls me across the floor and indicates with his eyes which one is his date. *She's flawless.* I've seen her around the hotel a few times this week.

I'm just about to ask Diego more questions when the instructor shouts for us to switch again. I can't even see Tony in the crowd anymore. I was too busy being nosey and now I've lost him!

Feeling a gentle tap on my shoulder, I turn to see Margaret's husband, Frank.

"Care to take this old vintage model for a spin?" he asks with a twinkle of mischief in his eye.

Oh yes, I can totally imagine him married to Margaret. He is wearing a crisp white, short sleeve shirt and a flower in his breast pocket.

I smile warmly at him. "Gladly, I love a classic."

Frank takes me by the hand and we start to gently sway to the music. Our dancing doesn't progress much beyond a shuffle but I'm so pleased that he's even here taking part in such an evening.

"I had the pleasure of meeting your lovely wife the other day." I tell him.

"Ah yes, she's a real gem that one. One in a Million." He has the same look that she did when she spoke about him. *This is true love at its best.*

"How did you two meet?" I ask him as he twirls me under his arm slowly.

"I scratched her car with my motorbike. She was so mad she started yelling at me in the middle of the car park. She was the most beautiful thing I'd ever seen. That was fifty-four years ago and she's been yelling at me ever since. Wouldn't have it any other way."

I giggle at their sweet story then feel a harsh pang of sadness when I remember just how close their story is to ending. *I don't even know these people but I can't quite come to terms with the fact that Margaret's about to lose him.*

"Any advice for a happy marriage?" I ask, trying to swallow my emotions back down.

"Live every day as if it's your last, my dear, because one day it will be."

Thankfully I'm saved by the sound of 'Switch!' again, just in time before the urge to squeeze Frank tight and cry all over his white shirt takes over me completely.

"Mind if I have my wife back?" Tony comes and stands next to Frank with a kind smile. Seeing them side by side highlights just how small and frail Frank is next to Tony.

"Be my guest, you're a lucky man. I think I'm just about ready for a lie down." Frank pats Tony on the shoulder before disappearing into the crowd.

I grab hold of Tony and pull him in tight for a hug. I squeeze him with all my might and breathe him in.

"Hey, you ok?" Tony asks, concerned.

To be fair, this is majorly out of character for me in recent years. I keep hold of him and nod my head, looking up at him from under his arm.

"I really do love you. I want us to be ok." I tell him, sincerely.

"We will be." He kisses me on top of my head.

"Promise?"

Alex

SHIPWRECKED

I WATCH HER FROM AFAR, Sienna that is. I heard through the highly active staff grapevine that she had come down to the salsa class. She hasn't come out of her room much since she got back from hospital. I'm sure she's needed time to recover from her injuries, both the physical and emotional ones. I'm glad to see she's out and about now though.

I'm not attending the class myself, I have far too much to do. At least that's what I tell myself. However, I have managed to find a convenient number of jobs requiring my attention in the vicinity of the beach tonight, allowing me to keep an eye on Sienna.

Who am I kidding? She doesn't need keeping an eye on, she has more security looking out for her now than most celebs! Since the night I kicked Mason out I've drafted in extra security to be on the safe side.

I just naturally seem to gravitate towards her, it's something subconscious that I can't help. One look into those eyes was all it took to put me under her mysterious spell. Maybe my mother wasn't far off with her mermaid analogy, except perhaps siren would be more accurate? I only hope this woman won't lure me to an untimely demise.

From my spot on the periphery, I can see her sitting on a bar stool sipping her drink, watching the evening's events. She's wearing a sheer white cover-up dress over her turquoise bikini. Her gorgeous, tanned legs neatly crossed and her long blonde hair spilling over her shoulders.

Just in the short time I've been watching (instead of collecting cash from the till like I should be) I have seen several men approach her and ask her to dance. Each time making the hairs on the back of my neck prickle protectively. *Or possessively, I wouldn't like to say which.* But each time she politely says no.

I'm considering going over there and talking to her, rather than watching her from afar like some deranged stalker. I just don't want to pressure her, she's been through such a lot and I respect that, but when I'm near her I can't hide how attracted to her I am. That's probably the last thing she needs right now.

Turns out while my head was putting together a convincing argument of why I should keep my distance, my heart had other ideas and took control of my feet. I find myself standing next to her, casually pretending to clear the table of glasses. *Right, like the hotel owner needs to be clearing tables. She's going to see straight through this shit.*

"Not up for dancing?" I ask her, wiping up a spill with a serviette.

"No," she chuckles, "I don't think my rib cage could handle that just yet."

I can still feel the imprint of those ribs on my palms from the compressions. The memory makes me shudder. Visions of her pale blue face, looking dead on the beach flood my mind and I feel sick to my stomach. She can't possibly have started to process the trauma yet. *I know I haven't.*

"How about a walk instead?" I offer gently.

She nods and slides off the bar stool, causing her arm to brush against mine. Every part of my body gives her my full attention. *She's delicate Alex, she's been through a lot. You can't rush her.* It's a mantra I've become overly familiar with reciting in my head these past few days. Now she's in such close proximity to me again, I need to remember it now more than ever.

Sienna follows me away from the crowded dance floor on the beach. The further we walk, the quieter the music gets, until it becomes more of a hum on the breeze. As we round the curve along the beach, the hotel is no longer in sight and the only light is the reflection of the moon on the lapping waves.

This side of the coastline is more exposed without the hotel in its way and so the breeze feels cooler here. Sienna shivers and wraps her arms across her chest. Without thinking, I instinctively run my hands over her arms to warm her, putting me only inches in front of her.

"Sorry, I wasn't trying to...you know. You look cold." Despite the dim lighting I'm sure I see her blush.

"It's fine," she giggles. "I am a bit."

"So how about that dance? It'll keep you warm and I promise I'll go gentle and slow." *Shut up Alex. Great job on giving her time and space. I couldn't have packed more innuendo into that statement if I tried!*

"I don't know how." she admits shyly, although she clearly didn't miss the suggestive tone this conversation has taken, her pupils are definitely dilating in the centre of her swirling irises.

"I'll show you," I murmur, as I gently take her by the hand and pull her close to me, snaking my other arm round her waist to settle on the small of her back.

She has such a petite frame and the top of her head sits just below my chin. Despite how incredibly long her legs are, she really is quite tiny.

I hold her close as we start to sway together in the sand. The breeze causing golden tendrils of her hair to whip around our faces. Sienna rests her head against my chest and relaxes into me. I couldn't have stumbled into a more romantic moment, with a more beautiful woman. My over-enthusiastic heart is getting carried away and trying to override my head. *Sienna isn't ready for anything new. It's too complicated.* My head is in there somewhere trying to force common sense back on the table but right now, with the moonlight and the waves and the girl of my dreams, I'm not hearing it.

I'm not sure how long we stay like that, silently swaying on the beach together bathed in moonlight before she looks up at me. She opens her mouth to speak, then changes her mind and looks at the sand. I gently lift her chin with my finger so she has to look at me.

"Whatever you were about to say, say it." I say softly. I don't want her to hold back. If only I could crawl inside her head and hear her thoughts.

"I'm scared Alex." she quietly admits.

"He's gone, sweetheart. He's never allowed back here. I have the best security team. I promise you you're perfectly safe."

"No, I know. I don't just mean right now."

I crinkle my forehead not really sure what she means, waiting for her to go on.

"I'm scared of so many things. He *will* retaliate, he won't just let this go. I won't be allowed to just walk away from this marriage without consequences. I'm scared of what my life will be now and what to do next. I'm scared to face everyone and try to fix my life. But most of all, I'm scared of how I feel about you." With each admission, she speaks faster and faster in a hurry to get it all out.

"How *do* you feel about me?" I know it's selfish of me to want to talk about that bit first, but I can't help it.

"Confused."

Ok, not quite what I was hoping for.

"You make me feel calm and safe, like no one ever has. And I'm obviously attracted to you, but it's more than that, you draw me in. It's intense and I feel almost powerless to stop it."

I trace my fingers down the side of her face before running my thumb gently across her lower lip.

I know I shouldn't, but I can't help myself. "So what's the confusing part?"

"Less than a week ago, I walked down the aisle with another man, who then hurt me, cheated on me and I almost accidentally killed myself. All of that alone is a lot to deal with, then you show up like some sun-kissed superhero, save my life and take incredibly good care of me." She's taken a step back from me as she talks, distancing herself slightly.

"I still don't see the problem." I close the gap and take her hands in mine.

"It's all too much, too fast Alex. I shouldn't feel the things I do... I can't." She pulls away from me and turns to leave but I pull her back by the arm and it makes her lose her balance causing her to topple into me.

She crashes into my chest and I take her in my arms. I crush her against me and kiss her hard. Our lips lock together as I feel her resistance crumble. She grabs hold of my shirt and kisses me back just as hard. I can taste the fruity cocktail she'd been drinking as her tongue dances in my mouth. She's stretched up on tiptoes to reach me and the force of our kiss throws us off balance and we fall to the sand together. I keep my arms wrapped round her to cushion her fall, I know how bruised she is.

I try not to think about the last time I was on top of her in the sand like this, this is a very different type of intense. We're close to the shore and the sand is wet, seeping into our clothes as we devour each other under the stars. We're both breathless and kissing with such urgency, it's as if no amount of closeness would ever be enough. My wet shirt clings to my chest between us and her sarong clings to her legs which are now tangled in mine in the sand.

I roll off of her onto my side, in case my weight is hurting her injuries, but she rolls with me and is now on top. Her wet hair falls around my face and the droplets of salty sea water run into our mouths as we kiss.

Sienna is the first to break the kiss as she leans up off of me to catch her breath. Her turquoise bikini is wet, and clinging to her every curve. If it wasn't for her gorgeous long legs straddling my waist right now, I could well believe I was in the middle of a mermaid fantasy.

Sienna breathes heavily trying to get her breath back making her breasts rise and fall in the light of the moon. I reach up to touch her face but she takes my hand and stops me.

"This can't go any further. Not tonight," she whispers. "Sorry Alex, I need to go and clear my head."

Before I have a chance to argue with her, she rolls off me and stands up, attempting to straighten out her crumpled wet clothing. She looks back at me once, with such a conflicted look on her face before jogging up the beach back towards the hotel.

Shit. I blew it. I took it too far. Why do I never listen to my head? I'm left lying, in the wet sand, breathless and alone. This is turning out to be one crazy week.

Diego

INFERNO

LAST NIGHT DIDN'T WORK out exactly how I planned. Salsa is such a fun-loving, sexy dance I thought for sure Olivia would come around. *Apparently not.* Her group of friends kept her away like some overprotective mob.

It was a complete misunderstanding the other night. I need to show her that she means more to me than just a holiday fling, but I can't get her away from her friends. Time is running out. She will be leaving soon.

All morning I've been distracted by ideas for romantic apologies but today is another day of back-to-back clients. This is our busiest season, so there isn't much time to get away and try to steal a moment with Olivia.

"Rosa, can you check the bookings for me please to see what my afternoon is like?"

"Yes of course." Rosa and I have worked together a long time. "Looks like you have a last-minute booking come in for now, but I can't read the name properly, someone put their coffee cup on the booking form. Maybe Ophelia? Olivia? I don't know, it's all blurry."

Hy heart soars at the news. *Maybe I'm forgiven!* Olivia has come down to surprise me once or twice over the week but I've had to send her away as there have been clients around. *Maybe she thought if she booked in again then we could be alone?* I like her thinking.

I suddenly feel more positive than I have for days. Instantly I go to the storeroom to make sure I get the best sensual oils and some rose petals. I also grab fresh fluffy towels and some candles. None of these things are unusual for a customer treatment but I want to give Olivia an experience she will never forget.

When I return to the booking desk, Rosa tells me that Olivia has already gone through to the treatment room. *Somebody's eager.*

I knock once before entering, as per spa policy, and go into the dimly lit room. I can see Olivia is lying on the massage couch face down, under a towel, with her dark hair cascading over the edges of the bed.

"Hola señorita," I say quietly as I go around lighting the candles and spreading petals.

She doesn't reply, but this could be all part of the game. I decide not to say anything else yet as I warm my hands before dousing them in hibiscus and coconut scented oil. *The silent build-up is definitely a turn on.*

Placing my palms in the centre of her back, I slowly start to rub up and down her spine. As I apply more pressure, she lets out a gentle moan and my cock twitches in anticipation. With large circular motions I cover her back with the slippery, scented oil and feel her relax at my touch. After a few minutes, I can't keep up the pretence anymore that we are strangers. I run my hand along her sides, across her rib cage, towards her shoulders as I get low and whisper in her ear.

"Are you ready for me, my sexy señorita?"

The woman leaps off the massage couch, attempting to cover her modesty with the towel in the process.

"What did you just say?!" she screams in a panic.

Oh shit. That's not Olivia.

"I'm so sorry, I thought you were someone else." I say hurriedly as she grabs her clothes.

Holy mother of mayhem, this can't be happening. Alex is sure to fire me when he hears about this.

"Madam please let me explain, I thought you were my girlfriend." As soon as I say it out loud, I realise how ridiculous it sounds. I really need to stop digging this massive hole I'm in.

"Is that supposed to make me feel better?!" she yells on her way out of the treatment room door. She storms through the spa reception with me marching along behind her causing heads to turn. This usually tranquil place is now the scene of hot gossip and speculation.

"Please, what can I do to put things right? I'm so sorry, it was entirely inappropriate." I call at her as she continues her swift exit. *God damn it, this is a disaster.*

"You've done quite enough. Thank you. Your manager will be hearing about this!" That's the last thing I hear her say as she lets the spa door slam shut behind her.

I contemplate following her, but it'll make things worse. All I can do now is wait for Alex to call me in and fire me. *What a week! First Olivia walks out on me and now this! So much for living in paradise…*

Lunch time comes and goes and still no word from Alex. *He must know by now.* I continue with my day's appointments as best I can but it's hard to concentrate with the constant threat of losing my job hanging over my head. In the end, my conscience gets the better of me and I decide to go and speak to Alex about what happened myself.

Just as I leave the spa and turn the corner, Olivia arrives, *the real Olivia* and I almost bump right into her.

"Hola," I say quietly, still unsure just how mad at me she is. *She's going to be a whole lot madder when she hears about this morning. I'm such an idiot.*

"Hey Diego, listen. I came to apologise, I didn't mean to go off at you like that and then for things to be weird between us for the last few days. Can we talk?"

I glance up the corridor towards the lift to Alex's office then back at Olivia. I'm torn about which direction to go in. *Surely if Alex was that angry he would have sent for me by now?*

One look at Olivia's sad doe eyes and full, pouty bottom lip and my decision is made.

"Of course, let's go to the hot house, it'll be quiet there."

Olivia looks at me confused. "Is that some sort of strip club?"

I don't mean to laugh out loud at her, but I can't help it, the look on her face is priceless.

"No, it's where all the tropical plants grow."

Olivia's forehead unwrinkles as realisation dawns. "Oh, you mean the greenhouse?"

"Why do you call it green? It is not green, it is hot." Despite how long I've been fluent in English for I still don't understand so many choices of expression.

Now it's Olivia's turn to laugh at me. "But what grows inside them is green."

"Aaaah yes. That makes sense." In just a few seconds, our roles have completely reversed yet again.

"Come on," she says, linking her arm through mine. "Let's go see your hot green house."

Olivia's eyes widen like a child at Christmas when I open the door to the hot house. She has such an expressive face; I could never get bored of looking at it.

"Who looks after all this?" she asks in wonder reaching out to touch the petals of a vivid pink orchid.

"I believe the collection is Alex's mothers. He's the owner. But there are a few of us on the staff who enjoy helping take care of them as she isn't here much of the time."

"How do you know about plants and flowers and stuff?" she asks.

"My grandmother. She used to grow all sorts of rare flowers and would spend hours teaching me and my brother all about them when we were children. She taught us to love and respect all things in nature."

Olivia smiles and raises one eyebrow. "You're quite the dark horse, Diego," she says, wrapping her arms around my shoulders. "Who would have thought such a man existed? A hotter than hell masseuse with a sexy accent *and* a caring nature."

She slowly runs one manicured fingernail up and down my chest causing me to shiver, despite the humidity of our surroundings.

"I need to be careful, or I could be in danger of falling for you." She looks straight into my eyes and every single part of my body reacts.

"Olivia, I'm sorry about the other night, please believe that I never meant to upset you. I had no intention of not seeing you again." I tell her as I run my fingers through her long dark hair. "If I'm honest, I may be the one falling for *you*," I whisper against her lips before pulling her closer and kissing her.

I only intend to seal my words with a kiss and prove my sincerity but the moment our lips touch, the atmosphere changes. Fire and passion start coursing through my veins and the heat in the room seems to double. I lift Olivia and she wraps her legs around me, perching her perfectly round arse on the bench. I press up against her as my fingers tangle deeper in her hair and beads of sweat start to run down my back and chest.

"Diego, listen," she pants as she pulls out of our kiss. She places her hands on my chest to put some distance between us and rests her forehead on mine.

"I want to know there's more to us than…well this," she says, gesturing to our entangled, sweaty bodies. "Let's spend one whole day together with no sex, you know, get to know each other properly."

"Whatever you want, señorita." I nuzzle at her neck and draw out the 's' of the last word causing her to tip her head back and moan.

I step away from her and give her my best dazzling smile.

"No sex it is. I'll take you out tomorrow." I wink before turning and leaving her breathless among the exotic blooms.

Sienna

SHIPWRECKED

I CAN'T BELIEVE I ran away from Alex like that. *I'm such a coward.* Every cell in my body was screaming at me to stay but in the end, fear got the better of me. *How can I involve him in my messed-up life? It wouldn't be fair.*

I barely slept at all last night replaying what happened on the beach over and over in my head like some sort of stuck movie reel. Lying in bed my skin hummed everywhere he had touched me with a gentle vibrating energy. I barely know this man, but he affects me in strangely intense ways. We're like two opposite poles, powerless to fight the attraction. I'm trying, but I'm not winning.

By the early hours I give up on the idea of sleep and instead decide to get dressed and clear my head. Some yoga on the beach during sunrise should do the trick. I plait my hair and put on leggings and a t-shirt before going to the shoreline.

The sky is a vibrant orange this morning as the sun starts to peek out from behind the glowing ocean. Alex's nickname for me springs to my mind as I look for an ideal spot on the sand. *If only I were a mermaid, it's got to be a whole lot easier than being a human.*

I close my eyes and start to stretch. A fair few muscles still ache here and there but I'm mostly on the mend now. I block out the twinges of pain and instead focus on my surroundings as I begin my gentle workout. This place is heaven. The thought of leaving here and going back to face the real world is terrifying.

After fifteen minutes of yoga, watching the sun lazily rise out of the sea, I hear the crunching sound of footsteps approaching on the sand.

Alex comes jogging along the shoreline wearing shorts and a tight white t-shirt. *So much for clearing my head.* One look at him running Baywatch style through the surf has frazzled all the clarity I'd just gained.

Last night when we'd been here in almost exactly the same spot, we'd ended up making out in the waves like a couple of horny teenagers. *I need to learn more self-control around this man.*

"Morning Sienna." Alex comes to a stop next to me and puts his hands on his hips as he catches his breath.

"Morning. Beautiful sunrise," I reply, squinting up at him through the bright sun.

"Yes, I run this time every morning, it's the only time I get to myself." He comes and sits beside me in the sand and looks out over the ocean. "You know, the sky was the exact same shade of coral the morning I found you."

I pick up a few grains of sand and let them fall through my fingers, not knowing what to say. I don't really trust myself to say anything, my head and heart are not exactly in agreement when it comes to Alex.

Just as I open my mouth to speak, Alex speaks at the exact same time and we both laugh.

"Ladies first," he says with a smile.

"I'm sorry about what happened last night Alex." I decide tackling the subject head on is probably best.

"Which part? The kissing part or the running away part?" The corners of his mouth turn up cheekily as he looks at me, letting me know he isn't annoyed about either.

"The running away part, mostly."

Alex raises his eyebrows and theatrically clutches at his chest. "Mostly?!" He laughs. "You really know how to wound a man."

I laugh and playful nudge him in the ribs with my elbow.

"It's complicated." Is all the explanation I manage to offer him. *How can I explain something I don't understand myself?*

"So you keep saying but it looks pretty straightforward from over here." He leans towards me and captures some loose strands of my hair that are blowing in the breeze and tucks them neatly behind my ear.

"My life is complicated Alex, all my life I've been raised to play a certain role. My birth, just like my marriage was all planned with a purpose." I let out a sad sigh. *It's really kind of tragic when I say it out loud.*

"I didn't realise arranged marriages were even a thing anymore." Alex blurts out, bringing me out of my own head.

"It wasn't an arranged marriage in quite the way you're thinking. Marriage doesn't really equate to love in my world. It's purely a business arrangement. My parents have never been in love, they're just business partners. Everything they do is strategic."

"Don't you think that's kind of sad?" Alex asks gently, stroking the back of my hand in the sand.

"It's all I've ever known." I shrug. *Of course it's sad but I can't afford to think like that.*

"It must be nice to have the freedom to dream about such romantic notions as a happy, love-filled marriage."

"No one can stop you from dreaming Sienna. That's one thing they can't do."

After a long pause, thinking about what he just said I ask, "Is that what you dream about?"

"Being married and in love?" he questions. "Yea, some day. Some might say I'm already living the dream with the life I have here. They're not wrong but what's the point of it all if you have no one to share it with?"

I don't really know what to say to that. I feel like I'm standing on the edge of a precipice and allowing Alex and his romantic notions to get under my skin would cause me to plummet. *I don't know if I'm brave enough to fall.*

"Anyway, when you're ready to see how simple it could be, you know where to find me," he whispers against my ear as he plants a gentle kiss on my cheek.

Before I get a chance to respond he stands and jogs away from me, continuing on his route. He turns and calls to me as he jogs backwards a few paces.

"Have a great day, Sienna." He flashes me a smile that is brighter than the sunrise and then he turns and disappears.

ALL DAY I've thought about nothing but Alex and what he said on the beach this morning. *Could he be right? Could it really be that simple? Maybe I'm overcomplicating things. Then again, maybe I'm not.* Less than two weeks into a loveless marriage to a man who I don't even know the location of and recovering from a near death experience hardly seems like the ideal time to start a new relationship. *Ugh! What a mess!*

I phoned my parents again today to try and get through to them and make them understand what Mason is like and what happened but it's like talking to a brick wall. All they're concerned about is appearances and that we make it *look* like we're happily married, not whether we actually are.

For some unknown reason, I even told them what happened to me on the beach and my mum's response was "Heavens, you must've looked awful, I hope no one recognised you." *I mean, with parents like that, who needs an abusive husband?*

By the time evening comes I have driven myself completely crazy and keep changing my mind about whether to go and find Alex or not. I tried to keep myself busy by visiting the spa and gym and going for a swim but I know my days in paradise are numbered and the pull towards Alex seems to grow stronger by the minute.

I change into a floral summer dress and decide to go looking for him. I don't even know what I want to say when I find him, I just know that something feels like it's missing when I'm not around him, *a very scary conclusion.*

When I get to the bar, I see Jackson in his usual evening attire talking to some people behind the bar. As he sees me approach, he excuses himself and smiles.

"Sienna, lovely to see you. How are you?"

"I'm doing much better thank you." I smile back at him but my eyes are busy scanning the room for Alex.

"Can I get you a drink?"

"No, I'm fine thank you, don't think I'll be touching alcohol again for quite some time." I joke. "I was actually just looking for Alex, do you know where he is?"

Jackson smirks as he wipes down the bar with a cloth. "It's actually Alex's night off but he won't mind a visit from you, I'm sure." he says with a cheeky twinkle in his eye. "You'll find him on the top floor."

I crinkle my forehead, wondering what Alex may or may not have said to Jackson about us. *Not that there is an us.* "Ok thank you. Have a good night."

When I get in the lift, I can see that the fourth floor is listed as private and not open to guests. I hesitate and my finger hovers over the button indecisively. I remember what Alex and Jackson both said today and go ahead and press it.

The ride to the top floor feels like an eternity and I start to fidget so I check my hair and make-up in the mirrored wall to distract me until I hear the *ding!*

Stepping out into the corridor, the marble floor is polished to a high shine and my shoes click as I walk, echoing all around me. There are only two doors along this corridor and one of them is labelled 'A. Andrews' in gold italic writing. I walk up to the door and raise my fist to knock but then I stop and hesitate again. *Make your god damn mind up woman!*

I can hear music playing inside and I swear I can smell his intoxicating aftershave seeping through the door and soothing me like it did the day he came to see me when I got back from the hospital. I trace my fingers along the gold writing of his name then place my palm flat to his door.

I so badly want to knock on the door and go through. He's just the other side of this door and I want to see him with every fibre of my being, but I just can't bring myself to drag him any further into my mess than I already have.

Resting my forehead against the door and closing my eyes, I try to convince myself I'm doing the right thing and it's for the best. I take a deep breath and walk away back to the lift, taking one last look back at his door before I step back inside.

Tomorrow I should book my flight and leave Alex to his life in paradise.

Alex

SHIPWRECKED

WITH THE CURRENT distraction of Sienna around and my dad's strange behaviour, I realise I've been off my game lately as far as the hotel is concerned. A few things have slipped here and there and I've left Jackson to do a lot more than usual. I really need to focus and get on with doing what I do best.

I'm catching up with the accounts when there's a knock at my office door.

"You wanted to see me Mr Andrews?" Diego's strong Spanish accent floats across the room.

"Come in Diego, take a seat." I gesture to the comfy grey chair opposite my desk.

Diego sits down but is uneasy. I can see how worried he is so I'll make this quick. I don't want to drag this out and torture the poor guy any longer than necessary.

"It's been brought to my attention that there was an incident in the massage suite this week."

Diego nods, looking at the floor. He then takes a deep breath and looks me square in the face. "I'm sorry, Mr Andrews."

"The young lady came to me in quite an upset state."

Before I can continue Diego interrupts me.

"It was unforgivable Sir and there is no excuse."

"Diego let me finish. She wasn't upset about what happened. She came to me with this letter for you." I hand him a folded piece of paper from my desk drawer, and he frowns at it in confusion. "She felt so awful about how she reacted that she wanted to send you her apologies."

"I don't understand," Diego mumbles as he fumbles with opening the piece of paper. "It's me who needs to apologise."

"It turns out she had quite the crush on you and when you mistook her for someone else, she overreacted and didn't know how to handle the situation, so she ran."

I give Diego time to finish reading the letter. When he looks up at me, I can see that some of the initial tension has gone from his face.

"That's not to say that your behaviour was acceptable though Diego," I say giving him a stern look.

"I know, I broke the rule about no relationships with guests. It wasn't intentional, it just sort of happened. Logic seems to escape me when she's around. That probably sounds crazy."

I chuckle and shake my head. *If only he knew just how much I can relate to that.* "Well, it just so happens that I might know a thing or two about that situation myself and have some sympathy with it. I'm sure you've heard about recent events here?"

"I heard rumours of the girl on the beach Sir but I'm not one for gossip."

"Smart man. So it seems this is your lucky day Diego because a week ago my world was black and white and this would be an instant dismissal. However, you've caught me in a week where I'm seeing things in shades of grey and to do so would make me rather a hypocrite don't you think?" I raise an eyebrow at him, curious to hear his response.

"I would respect your decision either way, Mr Andrews."

"You're one of the good ones Diego. I'd like it if you stayed, just do me a favour and keep it in your trousers from now on whilst you're on my premises." I start shuffling papers as a slight smirk creeps across my face.

"Of course, Sir, thank you so much." He stands to leave but I'm not quite finished yet.

"Oh and Diego, don't break any more of my furniture." He opens his mouth to speak, but no words come out at first.

"How..?"

"Don't worry, Stan kept your secret, much to my annoyance but unfortunately your new girlfriend's friends were less than discreet about it the next morning at breakfast."

Diego nods at me with respect. "I won't let you down Mr Andrews. Nothing but professionalism from now on."

As Diego closes my door I sit back in my chair and stretch my arms behind my head. This week has been so unexpected in so many ways, I'm having trouble keeping up. I chuckle to myself at the absurdity of it and shake my head before knuckling down to start the invoices.

Olivia

INFERNO

AS PER OUR AGREEMENT, sex is off the table (for now!). Today's purpose is to get to know each other better, in a less physical way. So, Diego has brought me further up the coast to a beach sports club. *My. Worst. Nightmare.* I thought he was joking at first, until we actually pulled up outside. I don't do sports, or water. Nothing good can come of today's activities.

After parking the car, Diego takes my hand and walks enthusiastically towards the centre. He has the biggest smile on his face, this is clearly something he's excited about. I haven't had the heart to tell him I'd rather pluck my eyelashes out one by one.

To my absolute horror, when we get inside, it turns out Diego has signed us up to more than one water-based nightmare, the first of which being snorkeling.

"You're very quiet today Señorita, everything ok?" Diego looks at me with concern as he collects the snorkeling equipment from the guy at the desk.

"Uh-huh," is all I can muster up as I eye-ball the flippers and mask in Diego's arms.

"This will be fun, no?"

No probably not. I can't knock his enthusiasm and effort though. He is trying really hard.

I manage a feeble smile, knowing damn well once we get near the water, I won't be able to fake any kind of enjoyment. *Maybe we should have stuck to sex, I'm better at that and I can do a half decent job of faking it when necessary.*

Trailing along behind Diego like some kind of sulky toddler I try to convince myself that it won't be as bad as I'm imagining. We walk to the shoreline and Diego stops, setting down all the equipment in the sand. Without hesitation he lifts his t-shirt up and over his head revealing a bronzed set of abs and a washboard stomach. I've obviously seen him naked before but in the bright midday sun, he looks like a wax work from Madame Tussauds.

"Remind me again why we're not having sex today?" I ask Diego, as I fully appreciate the view.

"My beautiful Olivia, this was your choice remember. You wanted to know there was more to us than just animal attraction."

"Yea, I'm forgetting why that matters with you standing here in just a pair of swim shorts."

He laughs a throaty laugh and thrusts a pair of black flippers towards me and a snorkel.

"You can't be serious?!" I ask him, knowing full well that he is. "I'm going to look ridiculous in these!" I hold them at arm's length between my finger and thumb as if they are contaminated with something nasty.

"Are you always such a baby?" He cocks his head sideways and looks at me in a way that makes my insides clench.

I'm about to pout and stick out my bottom lip when I realise that will only prove his point further that I am in fact a baby.

"Fine," I huff and roll my eyes as I attempt to stuff my feet into the ridiculously big flippers.

Diego just laughs and goes about getting himself ready. How someone can look so god damn sexy in flippers and a snorkel is beyond me, but somehow Diego pulls it off. His snorkel is propped up on his forehead as he offers me his arm where I'm sitting on the beach having wrestled on my last flipper.

"Ready?" he asks, pulling me to my feet.

"As I'll ever be." I mumble as I attempt to follow him to the water's edge. *Seriously, how are you even meant to walk in these things? I feel like a drunk penguin!*

DESPITE ALL MY WHINING, sulking and general brat like behaviour, once we actually started snorkeling, I loved it. We had the most incredible time exploring under the waves, I had no idea Spain had such a rich array of sea life. It's clearly something Diego is passionate about, he taught me so much today about the fish, the plant life and the delicate eco-system. His intelligence only adds to his sexiness.

I'd like to say that I didn't think about sex at all during our time at the beach and that my full attention was on the sea life at all times but that would be a big fat lie. When something comes in packaging that pretty you can't help but unwrap it with your eyes. But to then find out that it's not just the packaging that's pretty but also what's inside is intelligent and kind, makes it all the more irresistible.

Today has achieved its purpose which was to find out if Diego and I could relate on a deeper level than just sex and we most definitely can. So now I see no harm in going back to having mind-blowing sex.

After several more water-based activities, some of which I could tolerate, some I couldn't, (Jet skiing is a topic I never wish to speak of again!) we call it a day.

Diego drives us back to the hotel and walks me to my room.

"Thank you for a perfect day, Señorita." Diego takes my hand and kisses the back of it gently.

"You're not coming in?" I ask, surprised.

"No, I am going to finish the evening as a gentleman. You wanted to know if I saw more in you than just sex and so I am showing you that is true."

Damn, getting turned down never sounded so sexy. That accent!

"I didn't mean we had to abstain indefinitely."

Diego laughs, "I think it is you who cannot control the urges. It has only been one day."

He might have a point. "I don't know what you mean, Diego." I smirk and raise my eyebrows, feigning indifference.

"Goodnight my beautiful, Olivia." He flashes me his heart stopping smile before walking away down the corridor.

"Goodnight." I call after him.

I close the door and lean against it with my forehead. *Oh screw this. Who needs a gentleman anyway?* I slowly count to ten before racing down the corridor after him to get my kicks.

Alex

SHIPWRECKED

"HEY DAD," I call out as I knock and let myself into my parents' room. They stay in the same suite every time they visit, which is usually twice a year.

I just saw my mother downstairs in the restaurant and she said Dad wasn't feeling well enough to come down so I decided to bring breakfast up to him.

As I walk in, I can see that Dad is still in bed, which is most out of character. He seemed ok at the salsa class last night but there has definitely been something strange going on with him lately.

"Hello Son," he replies as he props himself up against his pillows.

I set the tray of breakfast food down on the side and go over to the bed. "I thought you might be hungry."

On closer inspection I notice just how tired he looks and that he's a little off colour. "What's going on, Dad?"

My father pats the bed gesturing for me to take a seat.

"Alex, I'm glad you came. There's something I've been meaning to tell you for a while now."

My mind is racing trying to predict what my dad is about to tell me. Whatever he's about to say, I know I'm not going to like it and he's about to blow my world apart.

"Go on," I say, nervously.

"I'm sick, Alex. Have been for some time now." He looks at the bedding and then out the window. Anywhere other than at me.

"How sick? What's wrong with you? Do you need me to call you a doctor?" Questions just fall out of my mouth one after the other as my brain tries to process what I'm hearing.

"Alex it's too late for all that. I've already seen doctors back home. I have stage four cancer and there's nothing that can be done." He swallows hard and tries to control his emotions.

I think I can count on one hand, the number of times I've seen my dad get emotional in my lifetime. He's such a strong man and from a generation where men showing emotion would be considered a sign of weakness. I can't believe what I'm hearing. How can this be happening? I knew something hadn't been right, but I never dreamt he was *dying.* Even just thinking the word inside my head makes me feel sick to my stomach.

"Dad, I..." I couldn't finish the sentence. I didn't know how. *What is the right thing to say?*

As if he reads my mind, Dad puts his hand over mine and says, "It's alright, Son. You don't need to say anything, but I do need you to listen to me carefully. There's a lot we need to discuss before the time comes and I need you to be ready."

How on earth can I concentrate on the finer details of his final wishes when inside I'm still reeling over the news that he's dying?

"How long, Dad?" I manage to choke the words out but hold back the tears. If I break down now, there'll be no stopping.

"Not long son, not long. Now listen carefully."

OVER THE NEXT FEW HOURS, my heart is broken beyond repair as I listen to my father's wishes and instructions for when he's gone. By the time I leave to let him rest, I feel exhausted, both emotionally and physically. He sends me on my way with a memory stick containing a typed version of everything he just told me, which is just as well because there's no way I can remember all that, my mind is in pieces.

I close my parents' door behind me and I suddenly feel so lost and lonely in my own hotel. I don't know where to go or what to do with myself.

As I wander for a while struggling with my own inner turmoil, I realise that once again my body and heart have taken over when my head has been unable to function, and I find myself outside Sienna's door. *Why does someone I barely know constantly call to me like a homing beacon?*

I know she came to my room last night and then changed her mind and left. I saw her on the CCTV. Before I got the news about my dad, I was preoccupied with trying to work out what had made her change her mind and leave but now I just want to be near her.

I knock on her room door, not knowing if she's even there but she opens the door with an initial bright smile when she sees it's me but then her face falls when she takes a good look at me.

"Alex, what's wrong?" she asks, her aqua eyes full of concern.

"Can I come in?" I ask her sadly.

"Of course." Sienna steps out the way and ushers me through the doorway, guiding me to the sofa. We take a seat together and she pulls me in for a hug. As she does so, I can't keep a check on my emotions anymore and I start to cry. Something about her just makes me feel comfortable enough to let her see me at my lowest.

As I tell her everything that just happened, Sienna doesn't say a word. She just listens while I lay with my head in her lap and strokes my hair and stubble as I talk. It's the most soothing thing. She never once interrupts me or tries to pretend to know what I'm going through.

When I'm finally done, I look up at her beautiful face. "Say something, Sienna. What am I going to do?" I say softly.

She leans over me and plants a gentle kiss on my lips, her blonde hair spilling all over my face.

"I think you're the bravest man I've ever met," she whispers against my lips.

I stifle a chuckle. "Hardly, I've just laid in your lap and cried like a baby for hours. Going on and on about my problems as if you're my therapist."

"Exactly," she says, without missing a beat. "That took a lot of courage to share all that with me. Thank you."

This woman is incredible. The more days that she's here, the more I'm starting to buy into my mother's theory about Sienna being here for a reason. I hope to God that reason is me because I'm starting to not be able to imagine life without her.

I kiss her back slowly and tenderly. The kind of kiss that is more about the joining of souls than bodies.

After the day I've had I feel exhausted in every way, but Sienna is so much comfort. I hadn't even noticed how late it had gotten until I realise it's started to get dark. Sienna and I have spent hours together talking.

"Stay with me tonight?" she asks quietly in my ear as she wraps her arms around my neck. "Not like that, just to sleep," she clarifies. "You make me feel safe, Alex."

Without a word I scoop her up and carry her to the bed before laying her down in bed on her side and scooching in behind her. I wrap my arms around her and she snuggles backwards against me. Within minutes we both fall fast asleep.

Claire

OCEAN'S APART

I CAN'T STOP SMILING. I'm pretty sure I woke up like it. An actual ear to ear, face splitting smile. The feeling is so unfamiliar that I'm starting to get jaw ache. After we got back from the salsa class last night, Tony and I had the most incredible night. We had sex multiple times like it was going out of fashion. We've *never* done that before. Not even in the early days when things were new and exciting.

Being here on this holiday, away from work has turned out to be the best decision ever. It's like a fog has been lifted for us both and we can finally see clearly what's been there all along. I'm not naïve enough to think everything is magically fixed, (we still have work to do) but things are certainly going in the right direction.

I'm still lying in bed when Tony returns from the shower wearing nothing other than a white fluffy towel round his waist. The white towel highlights just what a great tan he's acquired since we arrived.

"Morning, Sleeping Beauty." He smiles.

"What time is it?" I ask as I stretch over to look at the time on my phone. "11 o'clock!" I say shocked. "We've slept half the day!"

Tony laughs as he leans over and kisses me on the lips. "Well, we were up half the night," he says with a wink.

I feel the heat creep up my cheeks as I think about last night's activities. That along with the dull throbbing between my legs is a physical reminder that it did really happen, and it wasn't just a dream.

Tony unwraps the towel from around his waist revealing in no uncertain terms that his mind is on last night too. He grins sexily and raises one eyebrow as he uses the towel to rough dry his hair. I'm just about to lean back on the pillows and enjoy the visual when Tony's phone starts ringing. The sound makes me hold my breath. This is the sound that has grated on my nerves for the past eight years and come between us, ruining any special moments we've had along the way.

I realise the reason I'm holding my breath is because I'm waiting to see what Tony will do, waiting for his reaction. *Will he answer it? He always answers it.*

Tony drops the towel and walks naked over to his phone. My heart sinks that even after all that's happened these past few days, the minute work clicks their fingers, he jumps. Tony picks up the phone and I start to get out of bed. *Might as well get dressed and start the day if it's back to business as usual.*

Tony switches his phone off and gives me a smoldering look. "Where do you think you're going?" he asks as he stalks towards me.

I could not be happier right now.

WHEN WE EVENTUALLY LEAVE OUR room it's late afternoon and we're starving so decide to go to the restaurant for dinner. They serve the best seafood here. I saw someone else order swordfish the other night and I can't wait to try it.

Tony grabs us a table by the window. The evening sun is streaming in across the table and bathing everything in a warm glow. Just as we're about to sit down I notice that Margaret is sitting at a small table in the corner by herself, staring intently into a cup of coffee.

"I'll be right back," I tell Tony, kissing him on the cheek.

"Hello Margaret,'" I say softly as I approach her table. I don't want to startle her. "Is everything ok?"

Margaret looks up from her cup and smiles warmly at me. She looks tired today. "Hello dear, so nice to see you again."

"How's your husband doing? I had the pleasure of meeting him last night." I perch on the edge of the spare seat and give Margaret's hand a gentle squeeze.

Margaret smiles at the mention of her husband. "Yes I saw him take you for a twirl. Always a charmer that one. He's not so good today I'm afraid. He hasn't been able to get out of bed."

"I'm so sorry. Is there anything we can do to help?"

"No, thank you dear but that's ever so kind of you. Concentrate on having a wonderful holiday."

She looks at me properly for a moment and studies my face. "Speaking of which, you look different somehow. Happier, lighter...am I sensing maybe that paradise has started to work its magic?"

Despite how desperately sad I feel for Margaret and Frank I can't help but smile at her observation. "I don't think it was paradise, I think it was you. Yes, things have been much better the past few days. Thank you so much."

"Pfft," she scoffs. "It was nothing to do with me. This was all you two." She gives me a cheeky wink and starts to stand up. "Anyway, you two enjoy your evening. I'm going to check on my Frank."

"Who was that?" Tony asks when I go back to our table and sit down.

"A very special lady, who we owe a lot of thanks to." I reply.

Tony gives me a confused look as he sips his beer.

"I'll explain it all to you some time. Now what are we ordering? I'm starving."

Alex

SHIPWRECKED

WAKING up next to Sienna having literally slept with her and nothing more is a strange feeling. This is unchartered territory for me. *What do you say to someone the morning after when it isn't really the morning after?*

Thankfully there seems to be no awkwardness between us and so we agree to meet for dinner this evening away from here. I've got a busy day ahead with the hotel and my dad, so I kiss her goodbye and reluctantly start my day.

I'VE BROUGHT Sienna to a little local seafood restaurant just up the coast. I don't want to be too far from Dad and this place does seafood even better than we do (not that I'd ever admit that to anyone.)

"So how do you know Jackson?" Sienna asks as we take our seats at a table by the window.

"We served together in Iraq."

"You're ex-military?" she asks, surprised.

I chuckle at her facial expression. "Didn't have me pegged as a soldier boy?"

"No, not at all. You're both so... calm."

"It goes with the territory. We wouldn't have made very good soldiers if we didn't stay calm under pressure." It's been a long time since I've talked about my army days. It's something I try to keep buried, there are too many memories that haunt me.

Sienna nods. "That makes sense."

A waiter comes and takes our drink order, leaving us a menu each. "Will you tell me about it?" she asks, glancing up from her menu.

I take a deep breath and wonder where to start. "I enlisted when I was eighteen for lack of any better ideas. I was a bit of a tear away at school and had a lot of pent-up energy to get rid of."

"That sounds a bit of a drastic way to burn excess energy. Couldn't you have just taken up boxing or something?"

Laughing to myself I can see her point. It was pretty drastic. "I met Jackson really early on. We were in the same regiment and got on like a house on fire. When we were deployed to Iraq we went through hell together. He's always had my back and I've always had his, serving together unites people on a level that's hard to explain."

Sienna chews on her lip thoughtfully and nods while she thinks over what I'm telling her. It must be hard to imagine something so far removed from your own life experiences.

"Do you have any injuries?" she asks almost shyly.

"No, I was one of the lucky ones. Jackson unfortunately does. He has a nasty scar on his leg where he was hit by shrapnel. He's fine now but his leg has never been as strong as it was. You'll notice that no matter how hot it gets here, he never wears shorts. He doesn't like it when people stare at his leg."

"That's such a shame. Poor Jackson. Were you there when it happened?"

"I was the one who held the wound shut until medics could get to him. He was losing a lot of blood."

"Wow, that's incredible." A sudden moment of realisation flashes across Sienna's face. "That's how you knew how to save me on the beach that day isn't it?"

"Yes." I smile at her. "First aid and life support are all part of the training."

I don't say anything else. I'm not used to talking about this, not that I mind Sienna asking. I wait to see if she has any more questions.

"So how did you both end up here?"

This memory is a bittersweet one and makes me smile. "A group of us used to play poker at night sometimes in our camp. This one night we were celebrating a victory so had a bit to drink and we got carried away with the stakes. One of the guys, known as Paradise, bet the Spanish hotel his grandfather had left him. He had no clue how to run a hotel and didn't know what to do with the place, so he offered it up as winnings."

The waiter comes back with our drinks and to take our order, but we've been so busy talking we haven't even looked properly. I order for the both of us as I know what's good here and Sienna is happy to take my lead.

"Hang on," Sienna interrupts, "Before you carry on, why was he called Paradise?"

I chuckle, not at her question but at the realisation that I don't really know for sure. "We all used to have nicknames, I don't really know why his was Paradise, probably because he was dark haired and exotic looking."

"So, what was yours?"

"Promise not to laugh?" I watch as she holds out her pinky finger.

Linking it with mine, she says, "Promise."

"Duracell."

Sienna puffs her cheeks out in an effort to contain her laughter. "Why?"

"Because my initials are AA like the battery, and I had so much energy all the time."

"Makes sense," she replies through stifled giggles. "So what was Jackson's?"

"That is a secret I'll take to my grave. He made me promise never to tell a soul and I don't break a promise, especially not to a brother."

Sienna nods understandingly. "What happened next at the poker game?"

"Nothing, I won and we all went to bed pretty tipsy. The following day I woke up and thought no more of it. I never intended to take his inheritance from him, regardless of whether he wanted the hotel or not, it was still his. I was never going to cash in on my winnings. A few days later we got ambushed and Paradise was shot through the chest and died instantly."

I pause for a second to compose myself. It's been a long time since I've re-lived this.

"I'm so sorry, Alex, that's so sad." Sienna stretches across the table to reach for my hand.

"Anyway, it turned out the very next day after the poker game he had phoned home to make the necessary arrangements for the hotel to be transferred over to me.

When we finished the tour, I asked Jackson if he'd come work for me. He had no one to go home to as he'd been in the care system before enlisting so he agreed willingly. And the rest is history as they say."

"So that's why it's called The Paradise Hotel. You named it after him."

I nod as the waiter puts our plates down in front of us. The smell of the fresh seafood is mouth-watering.

"This looks delicious," Sienna says as she twirls a piece of spaghetti round her fork.

By the end of the meal, I think we have pretty much talked about everything there is to talk about and it's now dark outside.

I realise how nice it's been to take the night off and get away from the stress and bustle of the hotel. As much as I love it, I'd forgotten just how much I could do with the down time. Not to mention the worry of my dad. This evening has been a very welcomed distraction and I don't really want it to end.

"Shall we take a walk along the harbour?" I ask her.

"Yes, that sounds lovely."

I link my arm through hers as we leave the restaurant and make our way along the wooden decking of the dock. The edge is draped in rope swags to stop people falling in and overhead are strings of lights to light the path.

It's getting late and there's a breeze now, I feel Sienna shiver and move a little closer to me. After we walk a little way down the dock in comfortable silence I stop and take her in my arms. I don't know how she's going to react. Despite the undeniable attraction between us, the timing always seems to be wrong for us.

Sienna holds me back and looks up at me with those incredible eyes of hers. I cup her chin with my hand and lift her lips to mine. All the emotions of the past week or so pour out of me in this one kiss and Sienna takes it all willingly. She kisses me back just the same and knows in this moment that there's no going back now. I've fallen.

Margaret

SUNSET

THE DECLINE in Frank these past few days has been heartbreaking. He hasn't had the strength to get out of bed and he sleeps most of the time. Sometimes his breathing is so shallow I have to check he's still with me.

Nothing can prepare you for watching the life force of the person you love, slip away. As much as I was determined to stay positive to the very end and make the most of the time we have left, those things were all much easier to say and believe when Frank was still Frank. My once strong and brave husband who knew how to get us through any situation is now slipping away minute by minute. The only thing as devastating as watching Frank, is watching Alex fall apart. Two strong men reduced to mere shadows of their former selves within a matter of days.

Everything is in order. Frank is nothing if not meticulous and has everything taken care of. I think it's his way of trying to make this easier on us both.

Alex is sitting in the armchair with his head in hands. He pops in as often as he can, but he has so many demands on his time with the hotel.

"Alex, darling, you look so tired. Why don't you try to get some rest? There's nothing you can do here right now. Your father is sleeping. If anything changes, I will send for you."

When Alex drags his face out of his hands to look at me, his eyes are bloodshot, and he has dark circles under them. He's unshaven and looks a mess. He looks at Frank asleep in the bed then looks back at me.

"Maybe you're right. Jackson could probably do with my help by now," he says as he starts to stand up and picks up his jacket.

"Take some time out. The hotel will not fall apart without you. You deserve a bit of down time." I pat him on the arm, trying to make him listen.

"You should take that lovely girl of yours out for dinner. Spend some quality time together."

Despite how sad he is, a small smile dances round the corners of his mouth at the mention of Sienna.

"She's not my girl, Mum. We barely even know each other really."

"I think you know all you need to, darling. Love isn't details, it's a feeling."

With that, Alex kisses me on the cheek and smiles. "Call me if you need me, Mum." He kisses Frank on the forehead on the way out and gently closes the door.

"It's just me and you now Frank, exactly how it was in the beginning." I know he can't hear me, but I find it comforting to talk to him while I still can.

"Do you remember those early days before we had Alex? When it was all dinner dates and dancing and we didn't have a care in the world?" I smile at the memory as I take my pearl earrings out and place them on the nightstand. They were a gift from Frank on our wedding night.

Just as I'm about to get into bed beside Frank, my phone rings. I walk away as I answer so as not to disturb him.

"Hello Gloria, how are you dear?" My sister has phoned regularly since we got here just to check in. We've always been close and our boys grew up together.

"All ok over here. How's Frank doing? How are you and Alex doing?" Such a simple question on the face of it but with a multitude of complicated answers.

"No change from yesterday. He's still in bed, drifting in and out of sleep." I take a deep breath in and sigh as I watch Frank from the doorway. "It's like now he's put everything in place that he needed to, he's stopped fighting and is letting it happen. He's gone downhill so incredibly fast."

"Maybe it's just his time Margaret. It seems like he's made peace with it."

I smile and nod into the phone, even though Gloria cannot see me. A single tear escapes and slides down my cheek, despite my best efforts to stay strong.

"I just thought we would have longer." I whisper sadly. "Still, no measure of time would ever be long enough, would it?"

"No, I imagine not." My sister says gently. "How's Alex holding up?"

"He's a wreck Gloria. It's all been so fast for him to adjust. He only found out a few days ago and from what I gather, Frank bombarded him with all the details of everything he's put in place. Poor Alex hasn't had time to keep up. It's so typical of Frank to have thought of all the practical aspects."

"That's always been his way though Margaret. That's how he shows you both how much he loves you."

"Yes, I think you're right. Alex has met someone too recently. Lovely thing, she is. I only hope that the timing doesn't mess things up for them. I think she could be the one, Gloria."

"Oh, how wonderful. Life can be so unexpected that way."

We chit-chat about this and that for a while longer before she says, "Listen, you take care my dear and call me if anything changes or you need anything at all."

We say our goodbyes and I hang up the phone. My sister and I have always been close, ever since we were little girls. She's always been there when I've needed her, whether it was to scare off bullies in the playground when we were small or to listen to my troubles as we got older. Everyone should have a sister like Gloria.

After putting the phone away, I go back to Frank and get into bed beside him. He's laying on his back with his eyes closed and his breathing is so shallow that I take his wrist in my hand just to check for a pulse. It is still there, but barely. I snuggle against his shoulder and kiss his temple before switching off the bedside lamp.

The only light in the room now is the glow from the moon through the window. I can see the outline of Frank's features highlighted by the soft white light. His face is the most comforting and familiar sight in the world to me, I've been looking at it for decades. I can't shake the feeling that this might be the last time I get to look at his handsome face. I can almost feel him leaving me as the minutes pass. Just in case I'm right, I trace the shape of his nose, his eyebrows, his cheekbones and his lips with my fingertip in hopes of imprinting the memory into my skin.

"Goodnight my love, I'll see you soon," I whisper to my husband of fifty years before drifting off to sleep in his arms for what the last time.

Diego

INFERNO

THE LAST FEW days since Olivia and I smoothed out our misunderstanding have been some of the best days of my life. I've decided to take her to meet my family to try and convince her once and for all that she is so much more to me than a holiday fling.

We drive the two-hour journey early in the morning, chasing the sun as it peeks over the horizon so we can make the most of the day. I told Mama we would be there in time for breakfast, and we are making good time.

I had a very simple, traditional Spanish childhood. We didn't have a lot, but we were very much loved; my brother and I. Mateo, despite being five years my senior, still lives at home with my parents. He works in the family orchards, growing the best apples and pears for miles around. Our brotherly arrangement works well between us. Mateo stays at home so he can keep the family business going and to look after our parents as they get older, while I left to earn bigger money to send home. We both do our share in our own way, and it works, although I can't deny I do miss the more rustic lifestyle and the simplicity. The hotel is stunning, but it's so far removed from my roots.

As we pull into the dirt track that leads to my family home, Olivia gasps.

"Diego, this is beautiful! I can't believe this is where you grew up."

It's not much really, just a small white house with a terracotta roof but I guess it does have a certain rustic charm about it. There's nothing but orchards and fields for miles around. As we pull up outside the house, Mama comes rushing out to greet us with a big, warm smile on her face, wiping her hands on her apron as she comes.

"Diego, my beautiful boy! It's so nice to see you!" She envelopes me in a hug the second I step out of the car and covers my face in kisses.

"Hola Mama." I laugh as I try to fight her off.

"And you must be Olivia?" she says, turning her attention away from me.

Olivia smiles sweetly as Mama pulls her in for the same rib crushing squeeze she gave me.

"It's so nice to meet you, Mrs Santos." She says as soon as she is able to breathe again.

"Oh, por favor, call me Mama."

Mama gives me a look on her way past me as she drags Olivia into the house by the hand. A look that tells me she is more than impressed with Olivia already. *How could she not be? She's stunning.*

I grab our bags from the car and follow them into the house. The familiar smell of Mama's cooking greets me as I walk inside. No matter the time of day, Mama always has something cooking on the stove.

"Hola, Diego," Papa greets me as I drop the bags on the kitchen floor. "So nice to have you home, and you've brought such a beauty with you."

"Hola Papa, yes, this is my Olivia."

Olivia looks at me and a huge smile spreads across her face at my introduction. Papa's not wrong, she looks beautiful in her red summer dress and ballet shoes. I'm almost disappointed to have to share her for the next two days.

"Why don't you go and take your bags up and get settled while I serve breakfast?" Mama says as she fusses around with more pots and pans than one family could ever need.

I show Olivia upstairs to the spare room and put our bags on the floor ready to unpack. Closing the door gently behind me, I walk over to stand behind her as she looks out the window at the view. She leans back against my chest while I trace my fingertips up and down her bare arms, leaving a trail of goose bumps. With one hand I sweep her dark hair to one side so I can kiss her bare shoulders and neck.

"Mmm that feels nice," she says, turning to kiss me.

"Do you know what else feels nice?" I ask her teasingly as my hands head south down her dress.

"Diego!" she laughs as she turns to me, swatting my hands away. "We're in your parents' house and we're about to have breakfast!"

"I'm definitely hungry, but it's not for breakfast." I trap Olivia between my arms against the window and kiss her hard. My palms squeak against the glass as I press up against her and she moans into my mouth. Just as things start to heat up and I forget where we are, Mama's voice cuts through the moment.

"Breakfast!" she shouts up the stairs.

Olivia laughs as I sigh and step back from her, frustrated by the interruption.

"Come on, let's eat," she says, kissing me on the forehead and taking me by the hand.

FOR THE REST of the day, Olivia continues to impress my parents with her kind nature and her enthusiastic interest in everything they show and tell her. Even my brother seems to like her and he's not much of a people person.

I sit on the veranda next to Mateo drinking a beer, watching Mama teach Olivia how to make homemade lemonade. *I could get used to this. This slower-paced family life with Olivia.*

Mateo's voice brings me out of my daydream. "So where did you meet a fancy English chica like that?" he says gesturing towards Olivia with his beer bottle.

"She's on holiday. She came to the spa for a massage."

"Diego, you old dog! Fraternising with the customers." He tuts and shakes his head; I can tell he's only joking though from the goofy grin on his face.

"Sucks that she's only on holiday though. That'll break Mama's heart."

I look out across the grass where Mama is currently clapping at Olivia as she attempts to squeeze the life out of yet another lemon, just the way she's been shown. *I don't think I've ever seen Mama look so happy. She's always wanted a girl around.*

"Not just Mama's," I say under my breath, a little louder than I meant to.

"Oh Diego, got it that bad, huh?" Mateo roughly squeezes my shoulder. "You've got to fight for her, if she's what you want."

I sit quietly for the rest of the afternoon watching everyone else while I sip my beer and let Mateo's words sink in. *I know he's right.*

ONCE EVERYONE HAS GONE to sleep for the night, Olivia climbs into bed next to me and snuggles into my chest.

"I've had such a nice day," she sighs happily.

I stroke her raven black hair off her face and admire just how beautiful she is.

"Olivia…" I start but her phone starts to ping and vibrate on the nightstand. The reception comes and goes a lot here so often a backlog of messages and calls will come through at once.

"Hold that thought," she says reaching across and unplugging her phone. "Ugh," She rolls her eyes and tosses the phone away. "It's endless messages from my so-called friends. They're pissed off I've come here with you instead of spending time with them. I don't know why, it's not like they're even that nice to me when I'm there."

Olivia huffs and snuggles back down into the space she was in, tucked under my arm.

"Why do you put up with them Olivia?"

"I don't know, habit I guess." She shrugs. "I didn't have many friends when I was little, I was always the 'fat kid.'" She says using air quotes to accentuate her point. "I met them in college and it's just kind of been that way ever since."

Olivia traces her finger round in circles across my chest. "I know they're no good for me," she continues. "But I was just glad to be noticed in the beginning."

I sit up on my elbows so I can look straight into her eyes. "I notice you, Olivia. I've noticed you from the second you stepped into my massage room." I kiss her gently on the lips. "I'll never stop noticing you."

Olivia trails a line of gentle kisses along my jawline from the corner of my mouth up to my ear. It feels so good, it's distracting me from what I want to say.

"Listen, about when your holiday ends…," I start to say but she silences me by placing her lips over mine.

"Sshh," she whispers. "Let's not spoil a perfect day with talk of that." Her tongue tangles with mine and I can taste her minty toothpaste. The memory of what I wanted to talk about disappears completely as she climbs over me straddling my waist.

"Call me Señorita and make love to me Diego."

"Your wish is my command… Señorita."

Alex

SHIPWRECKED

I LOOK at my father's face for the last time as I cover him over with the crisp white bedsheet. Dad passed away peacefully in his sleep during the night. Mum rang up to my room during the early hours when she woke to find him not breathing. We've sat together in a state of stunned silence and numbness, not really knowing what to do first. Strangely, I haven't even cried yet, I don't think the reality of it all has sunk in.

We're waiting for the doctor to come to pronounce the death when Jackson knocks on the door.

"So sorry, boss. What can I do to help?" he says sadly, looking between me and Mum.

"I think we've got it all covered up here, thanks Jackson." I clap him on the back, it's the closest thing I can do right now to showing any emotion. "If you can just hold the fort downstairs for as long as necessary and send the doctor up when he arrives."

"Take your time boss. There's no rush," Jackson says as he opens the door.

"Thanks Jackson, you're a good friend. Could you have the kitchen send Mum up some breakfast please? She needs to eat."

Jackson nods and leaves us alone again. Mum is sitting in the chair beside the bed staring absentmindedly into space. I'm not even sure if she realised Jackson came in.

Most of the day comes and goes in a blur of phone calls, visits and information. By the time early evening comes, Dad's body had been taken away and Mum has gone to her room for a lie down. For the first time all day it's silent and I'm alone with my thoughts on my balcony with a glass of scotch on ice. The strong stuff. If there were ever a day that someone needed a strong drink, today was it.

I've never really experienced numbness before, until now. I can't really feel a thing. It's as if there are too many thoughts and feelings to process and so my brain has just decided not to. *Maybe I'm malfunctioning, like a computer when you open too many windows at once.*

My strange train of thought is interrupted by a light knock on the door. I glance at the CCTV to see it's Sienna. *Shit, I haven't spoken to her all day.*

When I open the door, she doesn't say anything at first. She just steps forward and wraps her arms around my middle, holding me tight.

"I'm so sorry to hear about your dad," she says softly against my shirt.

I smooth her hair with my hand and squeeze her that little bit tighter. Just her being here makes me feel better. *I think my mother might be right about her. I think she did come into my life for a reason, and this is it.*

"Would you like a drink?" I ask her, for lack of anything more profound to say.

"Yes please, that would be lovely." Sienna walks into my suite and glances around wide-eyed. I'd forgotten she hasn't been in here before.

"Alex, this is incredible. Did you design it yourself?"

I nod as I put the kettle on.

"Yes, do you like it? It's much edgier than the designs I went for in the rest of the hotel. This is just for me so I could have what I wanted. Coffee ok?"

Sienna smiles and nods in response, still distracted by the décor.

"I love it. Alex, you have quite an eye. I'm an interior designer back in the real world."

I chuckle darkly as I stir the coffee. "This is the real world too, Sienna, unfortunately some days it's a little too real."

She rushes over to me and puts herself in the gap between me and the counter. "Oh Alex, I'm so sorry, I didn't mean to offend you. It's just this place is so incredible that to me it's like something out of a movie, not a part of my usual screwed up life."

She looks up at me with those big, fascinating eyes of hers, that are not one colour or another.

"But it could be," I whisper as I bend over and brush my lips against hers. *I don't know what's come over me. This is hardly the time or the place, but Sienna has this spell that she seems to put me under whenever she's near.*

She doesn't hesitate or move away like I thought she would. She kisses me back firmly and tangles her tongue with mine. Taking a step forward I can feel all her soft curves pressed up against me and just for a moment I forget everything that happened today.

"I want to show you something," I say as we finally part from each other.

With her hand in mine and our coffee cups in the other I lead Sienna out onto my balcony. It's simplistic and minimal with just a glass barrier round the edge and a large round day bed in the centre.

I feel Sienna stiffen as her eyes fall on the bed. "Alex, I really don't think now's the…"

"It's not what you think." I interrupt her, cutting her off. "You're absolutely right, now would not be the time." I lead her to the bed and place both our cups down beside it.

"Lay with me a while." I turn to look at her so she can see my sincerity and that this is definitely not some cheap ploy to trick her into sleeping with me. I like to hope she thinks more highly of me than that.

Sienna steps out of her flip-flops and lays down on the bed as I lay down beside her. I hold her hand by our sides.

"Look up," I tell her.

This is my favourite thing in the world. Laying in the pitch black under the stars. It's like being under a huge black sheet with thousands of tiny pin pricks in it. There is very little light pollution here at night so the view is stunning.

Sienna gasps and I feel goosebumps break out down her arms.

"Are you cold?" I wrap my arm across her body and rub her arms.

"A little."

"Hold on." I say as I jump up and jog back inside to fetch a blanket.

When I come back Sienna is sitting up on the bed hugging her knees for warmth, so I wrap the blanket round the both of us and we huddle, drinking our coffee.

We must sit like that for hours, just talking and watching the stars. I tell her all about my parents and share memories of my childhood with her. I shed tears for my dad and she just listens and comforts me. She tells me more about her family and the heavy expectations of her and how her awful marriage came to be.

All of a sudden the brightest shooting star lights up the sky as it races overhead.

I chuckle slightly in shock. "Do you know in all the years I've sat on this balcony, looking at this view, never once has that happened before, until tonight? You truly are magic, my little mermaid."

I lean forward and rest my forehead against hers. We are sitting cross-legged on the bed wrapped in the blanket, both still clutching the coffee cups that have long since gone cold.

"What makes you think it has anything to do with me? Maybe it's your dad saying farewell," she suggests gently.

The thought makes my heart constrict. *What a beautiful notion.* Then I remember my dad's love of all things flashy and fast and it makes me laugh out loud.

"I think you might be right. It would be just like him to exit in style."

Sienna shrugs and smiles. "There you go."

She pauses for a second as if debating whether to say whatever it is she's thinking or not.

"Why don't you hold some sort of celebration here in memory of your dad? Something that everyone can get involved in whether they knew him or not. Like a celebration of life and all we have to be thankful for."

"That's a lovely idea. Dad loved a party, and he would like us to celebrate rather than mourn. Despite it being a hotel and people come and go all the time, I'm always trying to give the place a feeling of family and community."

Sienna smiles and snuggles into my shoulder.

"That's settled then," she says as she starts to yawn.

I don't know when but at some point in the night we both curled up in our blanket nest on the balcony under the stars and fell asleep. Despite everything that has happened, I don't think I've ever felt so peaceful.

Claire

OCEAN'S APART

TODAY IS the last day of our holiday before we fly home tomorrow. To say I'm not looking forward to it would be an understatement. This time away with Tony has been the best ever and we are like a newly married couple again, better in fact! I don't think we were ever even this happy in the beginning.

As we walk through the foyer to breakfast hand in hand, I see a poster pinned to the wall. I stop and read it out loud to him.

"It is with a heavy heart that I share the sad news with you all that my father sadly passed away two days ago." *Oh, my goodness. I thought I hadn't seen Margaret around.* "Oh, that's so sad," I say to Tony with a lump forming in my throat.

I continue reading from the poster. "As a mark of respect and celebration, there will be a candlelit gathering on the beach from 8pm tonight. All guests are very welcome, whether they knew my father personally or not. It is an opportunity to come together and celebrate life and all that's wonderful about it. Alex Andrews, Hotel Manager."

Turning to Tony I grasp his hands "We have to go, what a wonderful way to spend our last night here."

Tony frowns and screws his face up. "It sounds a bit depressing. I had more exciting ideas for our final night in paradise." He waggles his eyebrows flirtatiously.

Now it's my turn to frown. "We have a lot to be thankful for and I want to pay my respects. We're going," I say indignantly.

Tony gives me a lop-sided smile. "Your so sexy when you're bossy."

I giggle at him, despite my initial irritation. "Come on, let's get breakfast."

ALTHOUGH WE SPEND the day in the hotel today, not venturing out on any day trips, I don't see Margaret at all. I thought perhaps I might bump into her at the restaurant or pool area but she's nowhere to be seen still. During the afternoon we reluctantly pack our bags ready for our early flight tomorrow morning. *Back to reality.*

I turn to Tony as I neatly fold my jeans into the suitcase. "Things will stay better between us when we get home won't they?"

He stops what he's doing and pulls me close to him by my waist. "Claire, I've been happier these last two weeks than I have for years. There's no way we're going back to the way things were," he says planting a kiss on my forehead. "I was even thinking about putting a request in to work from home a couple of days a week so I'm around more. What do you think?"

A smile instantly spreads across my face. "I think that's a wonderful idea."

Once the bulk of the packing is done, we order room service for dinner and get ready to head down to the beach. I don't really know what the appropriate outfit is for something like this, so I opt for a navy summer dress and a white shawl. Despite how hot it is during the day here; it gets pretty chilly at night.

"Ready darling?" Tony asks as he links his arm through mine.

"Yes, I think so." I grab a handful of tissues from the side and stuff them in my clutch bag. "I feel a bit emotional already."

"Well, we can leave and come back up at any time," he says. I'm not sure if he's being sincere or hopeful. I decide not to overthink it.

When we arrive downstairs and step out on the beach it's already getting dark and there is a small crowd already gathering. Not really knowing what to do, we head in their general direction where we're greeted by a striking blonde lady with the most unusual colour eyes.

"Hello, are you here for the candlelight celebration?" she asks, giving us a warm smile.

"Yes, we are. Margaret is a sort of friend of mine." I try to explain awkwardly.

"She'll be so pleased you came, I'm sure." She reaches into the big wicker basket she is holding and hands us a tea light in a glass jar and a handful of tropical looking flowers. "Please take these with you and we will explain when everyone is here."

We thank the lady and make our way further down the beach to the small group of people. I recognise a few staff members so far and one or two guests who have been here all week. As I scan the group, I spot Margaret talking to who I assume must be her son Alex. I've definitely seen him around, he's ever so handsome and he has that air about him that lets you know he's in charge of this establishment. Not in a bad way, he just has that strong, silent vibe about him.

Today though as he turns and I can see him face on, he's lost some of his usual shine. He looks tired and sad, understandably. I don't want to interrupt their mother and son moment, but Margaret sees me and waves us over.

Margaret is dressed in a black sequin and beaded dress, with her hair fluffed to perfection. Even in mourning she looks glamorous.

"I'm so sorry about Frank," I say to Margaret as I greet her with a hug and a kiss on the cheek.

Alex excuses himself and moves away to talk to other people.

Margaret smiles but it doesn't reach her eyes. "Thank you, dear. It's nice to see you. You must be Tony," she says turning to my husband and grasping him by the hands. "Nice to meet you."

"Likewise," he smiles back at Margaret.

"Oh, you've got a good one here Claire, look at those dimples when he smiles."

I honestly don't think I'd ever really noticed before but now that Margaret mentions it, he does have rather cute dimples when he smiles.

I chuckle at Margaret's observation. Even in the worst of circumstances her character still shines through.

"If you'll excuse me a moment dear, I've just seen an old friend."

As more people gather on the beach, a circle starts to naturally form as everyone huddles together in their family or friendship groups clutching their candle jars and flowers. Alex clears his throat and taps on his jar to get everyone's attention. He's standing at the top of the circle with Margaret on one side and the lady who greeted us at the start on the other.

"As you're probably all aware by now, I'm Alex Andrews and I own this hotel. Two days ago, my father sadly passed away from an illness he had been battling in secret for quite some time. Some of you knew my father personally as you have been coming here for many years, others of you will have never met him. The most important thing to know about him was that he cared, deeply. He cared about his wife, he cared about me, he cared about the success of my dream at this hotel. and he cared about having a positive effect on everything he did and everyone he met. As much as it sounds like a cliché, he wouldn't want us to be sad, he would want us to celebrate. So, here's to an evening of celebration. Not just of my father's life but of everyone's. We would like to invite you all to light a candle and share with us something you'd like to celebrate before we all spend the evening dancing and drinking the night away, the way Dad would have wanted."

Tony gives my hand a supportive squeeze, knowing that speech would have made me emotional. *For a man I always assumed was never paying attention, he knows me incredibly well.* A pang of guilt hits me, knowing I've been doing him a huge disservice all these years.

Boxes of matches start to make their way around the circle as people light their candles and pass the matches on to the next person. As I light mine, a family opposite us steps forward and offers to go first. They tell us that they are here on holiday celebrating that their oldest daughter is now in remission. Everyone claps and cheers the little girl, who looks no older than around nine. She smiles the biggest smile and places their candle in the sand in the middle of the circle before dropping her flowers into the pool to let them float.

Everyone then follows the little girl's lead and each time someone speaks they do the same. As more and more people have their turn, the beach starts to sparkle with all the tiny candle flames and the pool becomes a perfumed soup of tropical flowers.

After a little while it's our turn to speak. I step forward clutching the jar in both hands and take a deep breath.

"I actually have two people who I would like to thank, because without them I would never have realised all the things in life I have to celebrate. Firstly, my husband," I say as I turn to look at Tony. "For not giving up on me through some tough times and not letting me push him away completely despite my best efforts."

Tony smiles and a few people chuckle at the last part.

"The second person is Margaret, who I only met less than two weeks ago but she inspired me to be a better person and to see what was right in front of me before it was too late."

I meet Margaret's eyes across the circle and mouth the words, 'thank you,' to her before setting my candle down in the sand with the others. Tony takes my hand, and we walk over to the pool together to float our lilies on the water before going back to re-join the circle.

"I love you," he whispers in my ear.

"I love you too."

Sienna

SHIPWRECKED

WATCHING Alex go through the pain of losing his dad this week has been heart-wrenching. *How can I be so affected by someone I've only just met?* I've been so caught up in Alex's emotions and trying to be there for him in the right way that I've barely thought about my own problems. But I know they're still there, lurking in the background waiting to be dealt with.

I eventually switched my phone off a few days ago and bought a cheap, new one in the town after receiving endless threatening calls and texts from Mason. I haven't told Alex; he's got enough going on and he thinks Mason is dealt with. *Boy did he underestimate him.*

Standing next to Alex now on the beach, I'm relieved that I made the right choice in suggesting this. I really wasn't sure it was my place, but Alex seems to be drawing on everyone's strength and positivity to focus on the good which was the whole idea.

We stand side by side listening to all the inspirational and touching words of staff and guests. Every now and then Alex's fingertips ever so gently brush against the back of my hand, sending a crackle of warmth through my veins like the heat from a fire.

It's so confusing to be so physically attracted to someone at a time of such sadness. I know he feels the same pull I do and is fighting it just as hard as I am. There's no rule book for how to deal with this situation or how to navigate your way through. It's messy.

I hear Jackson start to speak and realise my mind had wandered and I hadn't been listening to the last few people.

"I would like to celebrate this hotel and the success Alex has made of it. He's given me and so many others a dream job in paradise and for that I am eternally grateful."

Loud cheers come from several other staff members and the sound of clinking glasses as they 'cheers' one another. Alex smiles in appreciation but doesn't say anything. I get the impression he's not good at accepting compliments.

Eventually the whole circle of people take their turn and it comes back round to Alex again. Margaret takes a step back, gesturing for Alex to be the one to speak. He lights his candle and looks out at the sea of expectant faces.

"Thank you all so much for coming this evening. It

means such a lot to us, and it makes me happy to know there are so many wonderful things in your lives. I would personally like to celebrate the life of my father and also the strength and courage of my mother. Recent events have taught me that life can surprise us in the saddest and darkest of ways, but it can also give us exactly what we need in those moments too."

Alex turns to face me, and I swallow hard as he takes my hand. We've never shown any public displays of affection before, everything is still so new and raw.

"Someone very special came into my life at the exact moment I needed her, and she has lit up my life in ways she doesn't even realise." Although he's talking *about* me, he's looking straight into my eyes the whole time so that he's talking *to* me.

A lump starts to form in my throat at his words. He lets go of my hand and places his candle with the others but instead of floating his flower in the pool, he tucks it behind my ear instead, threading it into my hair. The look he gives me makes my insides clench and he manages to convey a million thing to me in that one look without saying a single word.

"Now, let's celebrate!" he shouts out to everyone on the beach. "Open bar for everyone!" The entire beach shouts and cheers as music starts to play and everyone breaks away from the circle to enjoy themselves.

I stand there rooted to the spot, still stunned by Alex's declaration as the party starts around me. Everything about him and our situation is so overwhelming.

A gentle touch to my elbow brings me out of my trance.

"Hello, dear. I'm sorry we haven't been properly introduced yet. I'm Margaret, Alex's mother."

"Yes hello, I'm Sienna," I say as she grasps me by the hands. "I'm ever so sorry for your loss."

Margaret smiles warmly at me, still holding both my hands in hers as she speaks.

"Thank you, but more importantly, thank you for what you've done for my son. Despite everything that's happened you make him happy."

I look at my hands in hers instead of making eye contact, feeling awkward from the compliment.

"It was him who saved me. I'm the one who needs to be thanking him," I tell her, although I'm sure she already knows what happened.

"I wouldn't be so sure about that," Margaret whispers in my ear as she pats my cheek with her soft hand and slowly shuffles away to talk to some other guests.

If I didn't feel overwhelmed by my situation and feelings for Alex already, I certainly do now! Margaret is so mysterious, and our conversation has unsettled me somewhat. Being responsible for someone else's happiness is a large weight to carry. One I'm not sure I'm ready for. *How can I make anyone else happy when my own life is such a complicated mess?*

When he's not near me, it's easier to think clearly and I know that now is not the right time for us to embark on anything romantic but as soon as he comes within five feet of me all rational thought goes out the window. The magnetic pull that I've felt since the day we met takes over and I'm almost powerless to stop it. *That alone is scary as hell.*

As I scan the beach, looking for Alex to see if I can do anything, I notice some commotion over by the pool. A group of women are arguing, and their voices are getting louder and louder. Jackson and the security guards start to move closer in anticipation of the problem escalating. I recognise the one with the long dark hair. She's dating the guy from the spa I think, who is also hovering nearby looking concerned.

All of a sudden one of them pushes the other and she loses her footing in her heels and falls backwards into the pool. Following the loud splash, everyone falls deadly silent and looks at Alex, waiting for his reaction. Everyone expects him to be upset or cross given the occasion, but his face is expressionless to begin with. Once he can see that the woman is fine and only her ego is bruised, he smiles and raises his beer, shouting,

"Pool party it is then!"

People take this as their cue to start stripping off to their swimwear and jumping in the pool among the floating flowers.

Jackson and the security team discreetly ask the two women to leave and sober up, but it mostly goes unnoticed as everyone is too busy having a great time.

I sidle up to Alex and give his hand a reassuring squeeze as he stands by the bar, sipping his beer and watching the party.

"How are you holding up?" I ask him.

"Is it awful to say I think I'm actually fine? This is exactly what we needed and what Dad would have wanted. He was always up for a good time and loved a party in his youth."

"I don't think it's awful at all," I say back, resting my head on his shoulder momentarily. "I think it's perfect."

Pausing for a moment to rearrange the flower behind my ear, I add, "Life is messy, loss is messy. Who's to say what's the right way to do it?"

"I think you might be right."

Alex

SHIPWRECKED

SIENNA TOOK my breath away tonight. In fact, she's been doing that since the day I met her. She organised this whole event and pulled it off flawlessly. She greeted guests like she'd been in hospitality all her life and somehow she just knew that this was exactly what Mum and I needed.

I've never been a big believer in fate and all the 'non-sense' my mother spouts, but Sienna has changed the way I see things. I really do believe that we were exactly what each other needed at exactly the right time. *We were meant to be,* as they say.

Watching her flitting about the beach collecting candles and glasses alongside the staff, you'd never know that she only had a brush with death herself the week before.

I put my hand over hers as she picks up another pint glass and gently put it back down. "How about you let these guys do that. You've done more than enough for one night."

Sienna smiles and shrugs it off as if it's no trouble.

"Come on, let's get some rest," I say draping my arm round the small of her back and walking back towards the bar. "This is what I pay these guys a fortune for," I say loudly in a joking way so the bar staff here me.

They laugh and roll their eyes. "Night boss," a few of them call out.

As we walk through the foyer to the elevator, Mum is there gathering up her shawl and bag. She looks tired but I think she enjoyed the evening too.

"Would you like us to walk you to your room Mum?" I ask as we come up beside her.

"Oh no dear, you kids get off to bed. Jackson is going to walk me upstairs, he's such a nice young man." She replies looking past me to see if he's ready. I know he won't be long, he's a true gent and never keeps a lady waiting, especially my mother.

"Thank you, Sienna for such a wonderful evening. You did Frank proud tonight." She pats Sienna on the arm as she speaks to her.

Sienna blushes and looks at her shoes. "Thanks, Mrs Andrews, I only wish I'd had the pleasure of knowing him. He sounded like a wonderful man."

"He certainly was. As is my son." she says with a smile and wink.

Mum says goodnight to us both and slowly makes her way to the bar entrance where Jackson is ready and waiting to walk her to her room.

Sienna and I continue down the corridor to the elevator and step inside without saying a word. I press the button for the penthouse floor, and it starts moving. The atmosphere in the elevator instantly shifts and changes to one of electricity. I watch the numbers light up one by one as we ascend, all the while listening to our breathing getting subtly harder and faster.

Eventually as we pass Floor 4, I break the silence. "You didn't press the button for your floor."

"Would you like me to?" she asks quietly, looking straight ahead and not at me.

I slowly loosen my tie and undo the top button. "No."

I hear her swallow and can see her chest rise and fall from the corner of my eye. I brush the back of her hand with the back of mine as we continue the tense ride to the top floor. I've never known it to take this long before but then again, I've never been so desperate to reach the top before.

As the elevator pings and the doors open, we hurry out of them and across the short foyer to my door. I swipe the key card and push the door open in one movement before pressing Sienna up against it as I close it with my foot.

She moans softly as our bodies meld together against the door and I hold her face in my hands. As our kiss deepens and our tongues entwine, my fingers accidentally crush the flower behind her ear, sending petals tumbling down our shoulders to the floor.

I lift her so she wraps her legs around my waist and walk her to the bed, not breaking our kiss for a moment. I bump into several things on the way, not being able to see where I'm going and Sienna giggles against my lips.

When I feel my shins touch the edge of the bed, I lay her down gently then stand there panting breathlessly as I drink her in. Her long blonde hair is splayed out across my pillow and she's giving me a look I've never seen before. She's usually fighting so hard to keep her guard up, but I think tonight I'm getting a glimpse over the wall and it's so fucking beautiful.

With hooded eyes and parted lips, she reaches for me and pulls me down on top of her by my shirt.

"Is it wrong to want you this badly at a time like this?" I ask her as I nip at her neck and run my hands down her curves.

"I don't think either of us have the strength to fight this tonight," she whispers back.

As I start to unbutton her dress down the front, Sienna gently tugs at my hair and sucks on my bottom lip, driving me crazy. When I pull her dress apart, I momentarily stop in my tracks when I see the remnants of the bruising round her ribcage, discolouring her otherwise flawless breasts. It's been almost two weeks since the CPR so I can only imagine how bad the bruising must have been at the time.

"Sienna, I'm so sorry." I say, tracing my fingertips over the yellowing bruises.

"I'm not. You saved me Alex. What's a few bruised ribs compared with never waking up again?"

She looks at me with such sincerity and I know she's right. I did what was necessary and I can't even begin to imagine a world where Sienna hadn't survived.

Instead of answering her I decide to lose myself in her instead. I gently kiss my way along her bruises and around the outline of her breasts. She sighs with pleasure and arches her back off the bed.

"I won't break Alex; you don't need to hold back."

The need in her voice tips me over the edge and I lose the last of my restraint. I've imagined this moment more times over the last two weeks than I care to admit.

She pulls at my shirt causing a few of the buttons to rip and scatter to the floor and I hastily remove my trousers. From my position, standing at the foot of the bed I undo the remainder of Sienna's dress and open it, displaying her gorgeously curved hips and satin underwear.

I know this moment is pivotal in our short but intense relationship so far. Our timing is somehow both perfectly right and incredibly wrong at the same time. Following Sienna's lead, I decide not to fight it for tonight and just *feel.*

I pull the tiny slip of satin down her legs and she shudders in anticipation as I widen them with my knees. Without hesitation I reach for a condom from my bedside table and roll it on. We both know if we pause long enough to think about this then we're doomed.

Sienna's pupils dilate as I lean over, making them look even more hypnotic. There are numerous things about Sienna that draw me in, but her eyes have to be top of the list. As I slide inside her we fit together like two missing pieces from a jigsaw that is finally complete. I'm no stranger to sex and have probably had more than my fair share of women in the past but nothing has ever come close to how I feel about Sienna.

We start to find our rhythm and I feel her relax into me. She doesn't take those beautiful eyes off me for a second. With my forearms either side of her head I bury my fingers in her hair and kiss her like my life depends on it. She kisses me back just as eagerly and pushes against me to increase the depth and friction.

Before long I can't hold it together anymore and I explode inside her, letting myself free-fall in the pleasure. I know it's the same for her because she cries out and digs her nails into the back of my neck.

I press my head to hers as we try to control our breathing.

"Sienna," I whisper in her ear while our chests still rise and fall together. "I think I've fallen for you."

She doesn't say anything back but I'm sure I feel a single tear escape and roll into her hair. We lay tangled up together, each lost in our own thoughts and watch through the window as a storm starts to roll in out at sea.

Olivia

INFERNO

AFTER THE BEACH clears of most people, there are just a few bar staff left collecting glasses and gathering up all the candle jars.

Diego and I sit side by side in the sand with our fingers entwined and I rest my head on his shoulder. Neither of us says anything. We know this is the end, I fly home tomorrow and I can't bear to leave him. I think we're both hoping if we don't actually say it then it won't be true.

I've calmed down after my earlier altercation with my friends, but I still don't want to have anything more to do with them. I can't believe they chose to get into a drunken argument tonight of all nights. Such disrespect for the owner when he's just lost his dad. I had to get Diego to help me convince security that I wasn't involved and shouldn't be kicked out too!

The multiple cocktails I've drunk over the evening are still in full effect and I feel like my skin is buzzing. Glancing over my shoulder, I look round to check the beach is empty and all the staff have finished clearing away. The coast is clear so I act on slightly drunken impulse and decide to do something daring so Diego won't forget me in a hurry. I stand up and drop the straps from my dress off of my shoulders, grinning at Diego while I do so, daring him to stop me.

"Olivia, what are you doing?" he hisses in shock, frantically scanning the beach for onlookers.

"Going skinny-dipping." I laugh as I shimmy my dress over my hips and all the way down.

Diego watches in open-mouthed shock as I take off my underwear and run completely naked into the water, screaming when the cold water hits my legs and stomach. Once I'm all the way in up to my shoulders I turn and watch Diego on the beach who is picking up my strewn clothes and placing them in a neat pile.

"Are you coming in?" I shout.

Diego waves his hands frantically, gesturing me to be quiet. "You're going to get me fired before you leave here."

"Well come in then and I won't have to shout." I holler extra loud to make him hurry. I know we shouldn't be doing this and Diego is right to be worried but I can't help myself.

Diego chuckles and shakes his head in resignation. He pulls his t-shirt off and over his head, revealing his perfectly tanned set of abs. He looks straight into my eyes as he undresses, playing me at my own game. Painfully slowly he undoes his jeans and pulls them off along with his boxers. He smiles at me the whole time with a wicked look on his face and one eyebrow raised. *Sexy. As. Fuck.*

Once he's naked he jogs over and joins me in the water. He ducks under the water and disappears. The water goes so still I don't know where he will reappear. I tread water, looking all around me for a clue as to where he is. All I can see is the moonlight dancing on the surface like glitter.

Suddenly Diego tugs my leg, pulling me under the water. I try to scream but the water fills my mouth, silencing me. When we resurface, we are only inches apart. Our dark hair shines like black ink in the moonlight now it's wet and mine clings to my shoulders in a black sheet.

"I thought you didn't like water?" he asks mockingly.

"It seems I'm willing to make an exception for you." I pant breathlessly from being dragged underwater.

Diego pulls me closer under the water and I wrap my arms and legs around him. Droplets of water sit on his dark eyelashes making him even more devastatingly handsome than usual.

He buries his hands in my slick, wet hair and pulls me in

for a kiss. The kind of kiss that makes everything south of my waist throb and ache. *I don't ever want this holiday to end.* I try not to let thoughts of tomorrow cloud my mind and ruin the moment.

Diego continues to kiss me and run his hands all over my body as we tread water together in the darkness.

A distant rumble of thunder stops us and forces us to take a breath. The rumble is quickly followed by a flash of lightning that lights up the whole sky.

"This is not where we want to be when this storm hits." Diego looks across the water concerned. "Come on, we need to get out of the water."

He takes my hand, and we make our way to the shore as right on cue another, much louder clap of thunder rumbles across the sky and a fork of lightning appears in the distance.

The sudden noise makes me squeal as we quicken our pace getting out of the water. Just as we wade out of the water onto the sand, the heavens open and it starts to rain, hard. The rain falls out of the sky so hard that it stings my skin. I scream and laugh as Diego and I run hand in hand back up the beach towards the hotel.

"What about our clothes?!" I scream at him.

"We need to dry off, I know where there are plenty of towels." He has to shout for me to hear him over the sound of the rain and the thunder.

Diego leads us round a side of the hotel I've never been before and in through a staff entrance that brings us to the spa. He punches in the security code and the door opens. As soon as we step inside, the lingering scent of lavender fills my nose and it's lovely and warm inside. Diego opens a large cupboard that is full of fluffy white towels and hands me one.

"Thank you," I say as I attempt to wrap it round myself. "That was unexpected."

"The past two weeks have been full of surprises," he murmurs as he watches me intently.

He stops rubbing his body with the towel and wraps it round his waist.

"I hope no one saw any of that." I giggle, suddenly feeling a lot more sober as embarrassment starts to creep up my cheeks.

"Seeing as fate has dealt us this hand tonight and we have ended up back here, what do you say we end your holiday the same way we started it?" He raises an eyebrow at me seductively as he waits for my response.

"Are you offering me another massage, Diego?"

"Yes I am, Señorita." He rolls the 'r' sound and draws it out to almost a purr making me shiver all over.

"But you could get fired from us being in here." I look around us even though I know no one is here.

"It seems I'm willing to make an exception for you," he replies, echoing my words from earlier.

Diego lifts me up on the massage couch and then leaves me to get comfortable as he lights candles and puts on music.

When he returns his eyes are dark and full of need as they graze over my body.

"Lose the towel," he commands as he pours copious amounts of massage oil into his hands. "I'm going to make this a night you'll never forget."

Alex

SHIPWRECKED

WHEN I WAKE up with Sienna still sleeping in my arms, the storm outside has calmed along with the one inside of me. I feel like I can finally see clearly and the clouds have lifted.

I know I have a long way to go as far as grieving goes and that it will be a long and complicated process but this morning, I feel better than I have in some time and it's all because of Sienna. She is the eye of my storm.

Not wanting to wake her I creep out of bed to the bathroom and dress for my run. The air is crisp and cool as the sun is starting to rise. My favourite time of day to run. I grab my phone off the bedside table and kiss Sienna's bare shoulder gently. She's laying on her front with her hair spilling over one shoulder and the bed sheet covering her from the waist down. My mother's mermaid analogy pops into my head and makes me smile. *She really does look like one.* I'm the luckiest man on the planet to have found such a rare creature.

I quietly close the door and make my way to the beach. I don't plan on being long this morning as I want to make it back in time to have breakfast with Sienna before I have to see to all my usual, daily responsibilities.

My run is refreshing and pleasant and has me feeling pumped up ready for a positive day. I try to get back up to my room for a shower, but I get stopped along the way two or three times by various guests and staff who all want to chat about one thing or another and pass on their condolences.

Eventually I make it back up to my room and peel my sweaty t-shirt off as I come through the door ready for a shower. A quick glance at the bed tells me that Sienna is up and awake.

"Sienna?" I call out. "Where's my favourite little mermaid this morning?"

Assuming she's probably in the bathroom, I head in that direction in the hope that she's already in the shower. *What a wonderful way to start the day that would be.*

No answer. The bathroom is empty and I can't find Sienna anywhere in my suite. *Maybe she went looking for me?* I walk back across the bedroom and take my phone from my pocket to call her when I notice an envelope on the bedside table with my name on it. *Shit.*

I feel the colour drain from my face as I open the letter and start to read the words.

My dearest Alex,

This is the hardest letter I've ever had to write. Please know that these past two weeks with you have been the very best in my entire life. I have so much to thank you for. You literally brought me back to life and gave my life meaning again. For that and so much more I will be eternally grateful.

But I have to go, and you have to let me. I can't hide here forever. I have to go home to face this and fix it once and for all. As much as you want to, you can't fight my battles and demons for me, this is something I have to do, alone. The fact that you want to run to my rescue whenever I fall is one of the many reasons that I've fallen for you.

We both have healing to do, you need time to mourn the loss of your father and I need to learn to stand on my own two feet without being held or pushed by a man.

When all that is done, if we are truly meant to be together then we will find our way back to each other Alex. I've left half of my heart there with you in Paradise and I will always be able to hear it calling me back to you.

All my love,

Your little mermaid, Sienna

"FUCK!!" I shout and throw the nearest thing to hand at the wall, which happens to be a glass bowl and it shatters to the floor.

I can't believe this is happening. How can she leave after all that's happened between us? This isn't the end, it can't be, Can it?

After several minutes of pacing up and down, dragging my hands through my hair, I finally get a clear thought in my head. She can't have left that long ago. There could still be time to change her mind. *Why didn't I think of that a few minutes ago?*

I throw on a fresh t-shirt and race downstairs to reception. I don't bother waiting for the lift, I run down the stairs, three at a time. Luckily there aren't many people about yet. I try calling her on my way down, but it does straight to answerphone.

"Sienna, please don't do this. Not now. Tell me where you are so I can come talk to you. Call me!" I plead down the phone to no one.

I arrive at Reception and march straight into Jackson's office where he is at his desk typing.

"Why the hell didn't you stop her?!" I yell. "I know you will have seen Sienna leave. You're the only one checking out this morning."

"You can't make her stay, Alex," he says calmly. He knew this was coming and he was waiting for me. "If you force her then you're no better than he was."

I open my mouth to argue with him but stop myself, knowing he's right.

"I can't just let her go. I have to at least try." I frantically pace the lobby trying to organise my thoughts. "How long ago did she leave?"

"About an hour, maybe?" Jackson offers reluctantly.

"Then there might still be time. I'm going to the airport." I grab my keys from the desk in a hurry.

"It's not a good idea Alex, let her go."

The look I give him stops him in his tracks, I don't think he's ever seen me this upset.

"At least let me come with you. You can't drive in this state."

I nod, knowing there's no time to argue. If I have any chance of stopping her, I have to get there fast.

THE TWENTY-MINUTE DRIVE to the airport feels like a lifetime. My knee bounces up and down the entire time and I don't say a word, too lost in my own thoughts to communicate. Before Jackson has even killed the engine, I leap out of the car.

"Find me inside," I yell back at Jackson as I sprint across the car park. I jump a few barriers like they're hurdles and narrowly avoid knocking over several people.

"Sorry!" I call back, but I can't stop. There's no time.

Once I'm inside the airport I push my way through the crowds to look at the information screens. I scan the list looking to see which terminal I need. *Damn it! Come on! Why can't I find it?!* Eventually I see Seattle listed as terminal five. That's where she's from so I'm taking an educated guess that's where she's headed. She said she needed to sort out her mess.

I take off again at speed towards terminal five but there are so many people keep getting in my way. *It doesn't happen like this in the movies! People part like the Red Sea for those guys!*

I see the huge number five in front of me and barge my way through until I'm faced with a security guard.

"Documents." he says, holding out his large palm.

"No I'm not flying, I just need to find someone." I tell him breathlessly after all the running, pushing and jumping.

"Uh-huh. Yep, I've heard all these lines before. No documents, no entry."

"Please listen, you don't understand!" I try to plead.

"Oh wait, is this some grand gesture of love?"

"Yes, yes it is, actually." I say optimistically.

"Well why didn't you say?" The security guard says dead pan.

"So, I can go through?"

"NO! Now step aside before I have you removed." He folds his arms across his chest letting me know in no uncertain terms that this conversation is over.

Fuck. That's it then. I just lost my only chance to convince her to stay. I take a seat on the lounge chairs to get my breath back and think. Sitting with my head in my hands, reality starts to sink in. *She's really gone.*

When I look up, Jackson is coming towards me with a questioning look on his face.

"We were too late. She's gone." I say sadly.

Jackson claps me on the back and pulls me to my feet. Neither of us really knows what to say. The crowds are starting to deplete as another flight gets called through.

On an empty chair behind Jackson, I notice a keyring sitting on the seat. Upon closer inspection I can see there's a small plastic mermaid hanging on the keychain. The kind you buy as a cheap holiday souvenir from a gift shop. A moment of realisation suddenly hits me. *She left this for me as a sign. She knew I'd come and she knew I'd be too late, she made sure of it.* I don't know if the gesture makes me want to smile or cry.

I walk past Jackson and pick up the keyring, silently sliding it into my pocket.

"You ok boss? Ready to go?"

"Yea, I'm ready," I mumble sadly.

The journey home is a quiet one. Sitting in the passenger seat I contemplate all what's happened over the last two weeks and how different life is going to be going forward. My father's gone and now so has Sienna.

I may have only just met her, but I was so certain she was the one. *Maybe she means it when she says we will find each other again, or maybe she's just letting me down gently. Who knows?*

When we get back to the hotel I go straight up to my suite. I'm not in the mood to see anyone. Jackson can take care of anything needed downstairs. I pour myself a stiff drink and stand on the balcony. It might only be early afternoon, but I don't give a damn. *I wonder where Sienna is right now?* I know deep down she's right, she needed to face her problems, but I was prepared to face them with her. Ever since I pulled her from the water and breathed life back into her, I've felt a gravitational pull towards her as if a part of me resides with her. *I hope she feels it too, wherever she is.*

"It'll all work out as it's meant to, son." My mother's voice makes me jump coming from behind me.

I was so lost in my thoughts I hadn't heard her come in.

"Sienna left. She's gone." I tell her as I drain the remainder of my drink and enjoy the burn as it slides down. I'll take physical pain over the emotional battering I've taken lately, any day.

"I know. I heard what happened. Everything is exactly as it should be. True soul mates don't stay apart for long."

I sigh and shrug my shoulders, not sure if I'm ready to deal with Mum and her nonsense right now. *And to think I was starting to believe she might be right!*

"What about you? How are you going to cope without yours?" I haven't missed the hollowness within my mother these past few days. She puts on a good show but she's in terrible pain on the inside.

"Like I said, it won't be for long." She gives me a warm smile and pats my arm. "I'm proud of you Alex, you're a good man and you've achieved so much. Your father is too."

Her words leave an unsettled feeling in my stomach, but I decide not to dig any deeper right now. It's been a long day.

"Get some rest Alex. Everything will be alright. You'll see." She kisses me on the cheek before turning to leave. On her way out she says, "Oh and Alex, let's give the whisky a miss during the day, eh?"

I roll my eyes and reach for the bottle as soon as the door closes.

Olivia

INFERNO

AFTER THE EUPHORIC high of last night with Diego, this morning feels extra flat. When we were done in the spa last night Diego dressed us in fluffy robes and slippers and walked me to my room. I wouldn't let him say goodbye, I couldn't bear it so instead we pretended like it was just the end of any other date. He kissed me with all the heat of an inferno and then I watched him walk away down the corridor.

Needless to say, after all the events of the holiday, the atmosphere between my friends and I is chilly to say the least. I'm totally done with them, it's time I found myself *adult* friends who know how to behave as such and treat me better. I told them to go on without me this morning and that I'd see them on the plane. They wanted to do some last-minute shopping before going to the airport so I said I'd stay here and check us out so I could have the alone time to wallow in my own self-pity.

I knew this was coming, it's a holiday romance for goodness' sake. What other ending did I expect? It doesn't make it any less painful though. Diego is one of the first people to ever make me feel truly good about myself and give me confidence. If nothing else, I will take that gift from him away with me back to my real life. *Things are going to be different from now on.*

Throwing the last of my clothes in the suitcase and wrestling it shut, I smile at the irony. If I'd realised just how hot it was going to be here and just how much time I was going to spend naked with a man, I would never have packed so many clothes! After a struggle I get the zip done up and go for one last walk round the room to check no one has left anything behind. I find three pairs of bikini bottoms, a pair of hair straighteners and half empty packet of cigarettes. *Slobs.* I shove them in my hand luggage so I can dish them out to the girls at the airport.

As I wheel my suitcase down the corridor towards Reception, I contemplate stopping at the spa to say a proper goodbye to Diego. I seriously consider it for several minutes as I go down in the elevator, but I think better of it. *It'll only make it even harder to leave him.* I decide to save myself the torture and keep walking past the spa entrance straight to Reception.

I check out with the receptionist and give back our key cards. She asks me if I'd like to write in the guest book which I'm only too glad to do. I give myself one last giggle by writing;

Best holiday ever! The Paradise Hotel is incredible and has the best spa I've ever been to. The staff are so accommodating and bend over backwards to please you.

I SMILE to myself as I sign with my name and a winky face. I doubt Diego will ever see my comment, but you never know. Taking one last look around, I reluctantly make my way to the exit, wheeling my suitcase along slowly behind me.

Bumping my suitcase down the front steps I realise that during my pity party this morning I forgot to call myself a taxi to the airport.

"Damn it," I say, reaching into my back pocket for my phone. It's not there so I try my bag instead. I'm so distracted by not being able to find my phone that I barely notice the black car slowly pull up in front of me and roll down it's driver's window.

"You going somewhere, Señorita?"

I look up to see Diego lower his shades and smile at me from the driving seat. His dark hair falls slightly over his forehead and the open white shirt he's wearing accentuates his olive skin.

I smile back at him; despite the fact my heart is shattering on the inside. "I forgot to book a taxi."

He kills the engine and steps out of the car. Casually he closes the door and leans back against it, propping his sunglasses up on top of his head.

"Well, that's just as well." He pushes off the car with his foot and stalks towards me.

I give him a quizzical look, not really following where he's going with this.

"Because I don't want you to leave." He tucks my hair behind my ear and rubs my jaw with his thumb.

This is exactly why I didn't want to say goodbye. His close proximity is making my knees weak, as well as my resolve.

"We both knew this day would come." I whisper sadly, looking anywhere but at him. "Don't make it harder than it already is." I mumble at the floor.

"But what if it doesn't have to?" He lifts my chin gently with his finger so I'm forced to look at him. "Stay."

Never before has one word had such a profound effect on me. Just knowing that he wants me to stay has my heart soaring even though I know that it's not a reality.

"Diego…" I'm about to tell him all the reasons why that is complete madness when he interrupts me.

"I love you, Olivia. I was awake all night wondering how to live without you and the answer is I can't. Stay. Please."

I'm not usually the emotional type. I've never been a crier, but I can feel my eyes welling up with tears at his words.

"And I love you, but what about my job? My friends? My life back home? I can't just never go back."

He wraps his arms around my waist and pulls me closer. His lips crash against mine and he pours the same desperation and emotion into our kiss as he did into his words.

After a few seconds he pulls back and says, "I'll admit I haven't thought everything through yet." His lips brush against my cheek as he speaks. "Just please don't get on that plane today. Stay long enough for us to figure something out." He takes my face in both his hands and pleads at me with his eyes. I've never seen him look so desperate.

It finally dawns on me that he is completely and utterly serious. "I don't know what to say. This is huge. You're talking about uprooting my whole life."

Diego interrupts my panicked rambling. "Say yes. Stay here, with me." He kisses my forehead, still holding my face in his hands. "Please," he whispers.

I'm elated and terrified in equal measure. My heart could burst knowing that he doesn't want me to go. The prospect of a life here with him is so thrilling I can't even find the words. Equally the thought of starting a whole new life is a daunting one. *Not that my previous life back home was anything to shout about.*

I nervously fidget with the zip on my bag as Diego's eyes frantically scan my face for some clue as to what my answer will be.

"Yes," I say quietly as if testing the word to see how it sounds. *I can't believe I'm doing this.*

"Yes?" Diego's face breaks into an earth-shattering smile.

I nod and laugh out loud at his reaction. "Yes!" This time louder and with more conviction.

Diego picks me up and swings me round in the air causing several people to look up at what all the commotion is about.

As he sets me down on my feet again, I place my hands on his chest firmly to get his attention and make him listen.

"But that doesn't necessarily mean forever. I'll delay my flight while we figure out how to make this work and what we're going to do. Ok?" I try to get him to focus but he's not listening.

"Yes, of course. Whatever you want. I'm just so happy you won't be on that plane."

I giggle as he scoops me up for another kiss. I've never seen him this happy and excited. He's worse than a child in a sweet shop.

"Give me your ticket," he says holding out his open hand.

"My plane ticket? Why?" I reach into my bag and pull it out, then place it in his hand.

Diego tears it to shreds and lets it flutter to the ground like confetti. "You're all mine now," he beams.

"I think I've been yours from the minute I stepped foot in this place," I say, looking back over my shoulder at the hotel.

"Let's go home." Diego picks up my suitcase and heads for the car while I stand there grinning like an idiot at his words. *Home. That's going to take some getting used to.*

I climb in the passenger seat as Diego puts my things in the back. Once he's in the car, he leans over and plants one soft kiss on my lips before revving the engine and driving us off to start our very own happily ever after.

Claire

OCEAN'S APART

"CLAIRE, wake up honey. It's time to get up."

I can feel Tony gently shaking my arm, but I refuse to open my eyes. Instead, I shove my head under the pillow, grumbling.

"No, not happening," I mumble from under the pillow.

Tony chuckles and runs his fingers up and down my bare arm. "We have to leave in two hours, and we haven't finished packing or had breakfast," he adds.

I slowly peek out at him from under the pillow, through my tangled hair. "But I don't want to go home." I pout and make big, over the top sad eyes at him.

"I know," he says softly. "We've had the best time, but unfortunately real life awaits." He offers me a steaming cup of coffee in hope of cheering me up and getting me moving. *Nice try.*

"Real life sucks," I groan as I sit up cross-legged on the bed and take the cup from him.

Tony laughs hard. "Apparently hangovers bring out your inner stroppy teenager. I wish I'd known sooner; I would have got you drunk more often. You're sexy when you're sulky and stroppy."

I pretend to glare at him as I sip my coffee. *God that's good.*

"Firstly, I am not hungover." I protest and Tony rolls his eyes. "Secondly, I'm not sulking, or stroppy or sexy." I try to raise one finger at a time as I list all the things he just said but it's too early and I'm too tired so I give up.

"Wrong, wrong and wrong again." He laughs back at me. "I gave up counting after your fourth cocktail last night, but I know there were several more. How's your head?"

I half-smile at him, admitting defeat. "It's felt better. I'm getting too old for this shit. I don't bounce back like I used to."

Tony gives me a wickedly sexy smile from behind his own coffee cup. "You were bouncing around plenty last night, the way I remember it."

I open my mouth in shock and swat his arm playfully. "Tony!"

"Ok, ok." He laughs, raising his hands defensively. "How about some paracetamol and breakfast to go with that coffee?"

"Sounds perfect."

AN HOUR and a half later and we are packed up and just finishing breakfast in the restaurant. I'm so full I can barely move.

"The taxi will be coming for us soon. We should bring our luggage down," Tony says as he enjoys his last mouthful of eggs and bacon.

"Can you manage on your own if I try to find Margaret really quick to say goodbye?"

Tony grins at me and flexes his bicep playfully. "I think I'll be alright."

Rolling my eyes, I throw my napkin at him and stand to go in search of Margaret. I love this new side to our relationship. We've never been this playful with each other before. *I guess we've never really had the time.* I'm determined to make these changes stick when we go home to 'real life'.

I recognise Alex standing in the foyer talking to another member of staff. I wait politely to one side for him to finish his conversation.

"Hi, can I help you?" he asks, turning to me. I can tell from his expression he's trying to work out if he should know my name or not.

"I was looking for your mother, Margaret. Is she around? We leave today and I wanted to say goodbye."

"Oh, yes of course. She's sitting by the pool I believe." He gestures in that general direction as his phone starts to ring in his pocket.

"Thanks ever so much." Alex waves a finger at me as he answers the phone. *That is one busy man.*

When I get to the pool, Margaret is sitting on a sunbed, cocktail in hand. (Non-alcoholic I presume considering the time of day!)

"Mind if I sit here?" I ask her the exact same way she did me when we first met.

She looks up and smiles warmly at me, causing her soft skin to crinkle round her eyes and lips. "Claire dear! How lovely to see you."

I take a seat next to her and she offers me some fruit from her bowl of fruit salad.

"No, thank you." I shake my head. "I've just eaten."

Margaret frowns a little. "You must make sure you get enough vitamins dear. It's important."

I chuckle at her and roll my eyes slightly. "Why the sudden interest in my health?"

Margaret looks momentarily flustered as if she's said something she shouldn't. "No special reason. It's just a good habit to get into."

Now I'm the one frowning. Margaret can be so mysterious sometimes. She also seems to know something everyone else doesn't. *Maybe that's just what all those years of experience do to you.*

"I've come to say goodbye Margaret, we leave today." Although I barely know this lady, I feel sad saying goodbye to her.

"Oh ok dear, well it's been lovely having you here. I hope you've enjoyed your time away. And thanks again for coming last night, that was kind of you." She places her hand over mine as she speaks and gives it a pat.

"We've had the most wonderful time, truly and that has a lot to do with you, Margaret so thank you."

"Nonsense. All I did was help you see what you already knew. Do you think you'll come back?"

"Most definitely! You try stopping me! See you same time next year for a piña colada by the pool?"

Margaret chuckles softly. "Sounds wonderful. Anyway, don't let me hold you up. You look after yourself now."

"I hope the funeral goes as well as these things can. Look after yourself Margaret." I lean in for a hug and notice how she smells of pear drops, such an old, classic sweet.

"Bye," I give her one last smile and wave as I leave the pool and head back to the entrance to meet Tony.

"There you are," he says pulling me to him round my waist for a kiss. "I was looking for you. Are you ready to go?"

"No, not really but yes," I say sadly, taking one last look at this beautiful slice of paradise as we make our way down the front steps to the taxi.

"This is just the beginning darling. Things are going to be so good from now on. You'll see."

I kiss my husband and we walk hand in hand towards a better future together.

Epilogue

ALEX

IT'S BEEN a year since my father passed. A lot has happened since then. In the weeks that followed I converted the suite next to my own and moved my mother in so I could take care of her. I made Jackson a partner so that I could work less hours and take care of her.

Sadly though, three months later, I lost her too. She died peacefully, but unexpectedly in her sleep one night. The doctors said she had an aneurism, but I believe she died from a broken heart. True soul mates won't be kept apart for long. I'm sure she even said those exact words to me once. She missed my father terribly after he passed away and she was never quite the same after that as if part of her was missing.

"Hey Alex, what's the ETA on that wedding party?" Jackson snaps me out of my daydream. I've found my mind wandering a lot lately. I guess it's been an emotional year with a lot to process.

"The main bridal party will be checking in at around half three," I reply, realising I've been absentmindedly doodling on a piece of paper on my desk.

It's only a black and white sketch but I know who's eyes they are. Even when I'm not thinking about her, *I'm thinking about her.* Sienna, my little mermaid with the colour-shifting, hypnotic eyes. Not a day goes by when I don't wonder where she is or what she's doing.

"I'm going downstairs to make sure everything is ready with the catering team. I'll catch up with you later about the plans for the new pool refurb." *I need to get out of this office and out my head.*

The hotel is fully booked this season. We've always been very fortunate and successful, but this year has been the busiest yet. When I get down to reception, the whole hotel has an energetic buzz about it. There is a large wedding party arriving today, and weddings always seem to make everyone happy.

"Morning ladies, everything running smoothly so far?" I ask the receptionists as I scan the daily log book for anything important I should know about.

"So far, so good," Harriet replies. "Oh, there was one thing. A couple were here asking for your mother. I didn't recognise them, but they said their names were Claire and Tony. I didn't know what to say, not knowing who they were so I said you would see them when you had a chance. I hope that's ok?"

"Yes, of course, thank you. Where can I find them?"

"They've checked in to Room 32, but I think they were headed to the bistro for a spot of early lunch."

"Thanks Harriett. Let me know if you need anything."

I make my way to the bistro, passing lots of happy, relaxed holidaymakers on my way. A few of the regulars greet me as I pass. Many of them come back at least once a year so I know them by name. It occurs to me as I arrive, that I have no idea what these people look like so how will I know when I've found them?

Scanning the room, I notice a couple sitting a table in the corner. They are fussing over a newborn. *I think I recognise them from last year. I'm sure the woman was talking to my mother at the candlelit vigil.* Answering my question, the woman looks up from the baby and waves at me with a smile.

I make my way over to their table. "Good morning," I greet them, not really knowing what else to say at this point.

"Hello Alex, it's so nice to see you again. I'm Claire," she says with a friendly smile before taking the baby from her husband so he can shake my hand.

"Tony." He offers, along with his hand.

The look of confusion on my face must be apparent because Claire jumps right in with, "Sorry to take up your time, I'm sure you're ever so busy. I don't suppose you remember us, but we were here on holiday last year when your father sadly passed. We were at the vigil; it was a beautiful thing."

I smile in appreciation and look at a scuff on my shoe. I still struggle to talk about my mother and father in the past tense.

"I do remember you a little. You were talking to my mother."

The woman's face lights up at the mention of her. *She doesn't know.*

"Yes, I was. Margaret was such a blessing to me when we were here, and she gave me some invaluable life-changing advice." She and Tony exchange affectionate glances. "You see if it wasn't for your mother then this little bundle of joy wouldn't be in our lives." Claire holds the baby up in the air and coos at it lovingly.

"Is your mother here? We came back in the hopes of seeing her and so she could meet Margaret, or Maggie for short." She gestures to the tiny baby nestled in the blankets.

Wow, they named their baby after my mother. I suddenly feel really choked and struggle to find the right words.

"I'm so sorry, she passed away a few months after my father."

Claire's hand flies to her mouth and she starts to tear up.

"Oh my goodness, I'm so very sorry Alex. Your parents were truly wonderful people. What happened?"

"They said a sudden aneurism, but I don't think if truth be told she could live without my father."

Claire nods sadly. "I know how very much in love they were."

There's an uncomfortable sad silence while everyone processes what's happened.

"Anyway," I clear my throat. "It was so nice of you to come back. I know my mother would've loved to meet Maggie. Why don't you join me for dinner one evening while you're here and you can tell me more about your encounters with her."

"Thank you, we'd like that very much," Claire says whilst rubbing soothing circles on the baby's back.

I smile and nod to say goodbye before leaving the restaurant. *My mother was always offering relationship advice and matchmaking. It would appear her habit extended outside of the family.* It's really quite touching that they named their baby after her. She must have made quite an impression.

When I return to reception, things have got busier with some of the wedding guests starting to check In. I can see the receptionists are all on the phone or checking in new arrivals, so I decide not to bother them and instead go back up to my office. As I'm about to leave, Harriet gestures for me to wait until she gets off the phone. When she's done, she smiles at me and says, "There's someone here to see you Alex, they're waiting outside the front entrance."

"Did they leave a name?" I ask distracted, I've just noticed a large shipment of new equipment pull up for the spa. *It's probably another distant acquaintance hoping to get a discounted holiday.*

"No name," she says as the phone rings again.

"Thanks Harriet." I decide to kill two birds with one stone and see who the visitor is on my way to sign for the shipment. As I leave the foyer, I put my sunglasses on to shade me from the morning sun. The heat prickles my skin instantly once I step outside the air-conditioned entrance.

I casually make my way down the grand steps at the front of the hotel to the gravel car park and there is a woman wearing a wide brimmed sun hat standing with her back to me. I'd know the outline of that figure anywhere. Upon hearing my shoes crunch on the gravel, she turns to look at me, revealing those hypnotic eyes.

Sienna.

Want to know more about Paradise?

Return to Paradise

Read the epic conclusion to Alex and Sienna's story and fall in love with a whole new set of characters in the stunning sequel 'Return to Paradise'

...Coming Summer 2022

Acknowledgements

There are a lot of people I need to thank for *Welcome to Paradise* to have come into existence.

In the relatively short time I've been writing books, I am lucky enough to have met some of the most incredibly supportive and encouraging people in my journey so far.

The support and positivity I received for *Rock Your World* spurred me on and gave me the confidence to write another book. So to all those who purchased, read or reviewed, thank you so much. You'll never know how much it means.

My amazing beta readers who guide and encourage me are so important. They do so much more than 'just read' as one them once put it. I would like to give particular thanks to Pat who doesn't let me wobble and fall when the doubt creeps in, but instead dusts me off, helps me up and makes me carry on.

The wonderful Krissy at Author Bunnies deserves so much praise for this book, there are not enough pages! Not only does she do a wonderful job editing for me and pointing out all my weird and wonderful mistakes but she also swooped in and saved the day with the stunning cover. In all seriousness, this book wouldn't exist without her!

A huge thank you to TL Swan and my fellow Cygnet Inkers for being the best support network anyone could wish for. These girls are always there to listen and advise with only encouraging words and never an ounce of judgement – girl power at its finest!

Last but definitely not least, I would like to thank my husband and family for their ongoing support and belief in me.

About the Author

B Crowhurst is a working mum of two from the UK. She discovered her love of writing during one of many lockdowns in 2020. Writing her first book on her phone at night whilst waiting for her son to fall asleep, she soon realised that writing was more than just a distraction from the crazy new way of life.

Ten months later, B Crowhurst published her first novel 'Rock Your World' and has never looked back.

For more information, find all B Crowhurst's links here:

https://linktr.ee/bcrowhurstauthor

Printed in Great Britain
by Amazon

79392543R00129